The Speed of Darkness

The Speed of Darkness

stories by
Rodney Morales

Bamboo Ridge Press
1988

This is a special double issue of *Bamboo Ridge, The Hawaii Writers' Quarterly,* issues no. 39 and 40, Summer and Fall 1988, ISSN 0733-0308

ISBN 0-910043-16-7
Library of Congress Catalog Card Number 88-24246
Indexed in the American Humanities Index

Published by Bamboo Ridge Press.

The cover art is by Santos Barbasa. Some of the stories in this collection might be recognized as slightly altered versions of stories previously published in *Hawaii Review, Ramrod,* and *Honolulu Magazine.*

———————

This project is supported by a grant from the National Endowment for the Arts (NEA), a Federal agency. It is also supported, in part, by a grant from the State Foundation (SFCA). The SFCA is funded by appropriations from the Hawaii State Legislature and by grants from the NEA.

Bamboo Ridge Press
P.O. Box 61781
Honolulu, Hawaii 96839-1781

———————

Library of Congress Cataloging-in-Publication Data

Morales, Rodney, 1952-
    The speed of darkness.

    I. Title.
PS3563.07594S64   1988   813'54   88-24246
ISBN 0-910043-16-7 (pbk.)

10 9 8 7 6 5 4 3   94 95 96

Acknowledgments

I wish to thank the editors of Bamboo Ridge Press—
Darrell Lum, Eric Chock, Mavis Hara—for their support in this
project. I'd also like to thank the following people for giving
their priceless time and attention to my work all these years:
Wing Tek Lum, Ian MacMillan, Lizabeth Ball, Ann Kamimura,
Philip Damon, and Holly Yamada.

—R.E.M.

Contents

for Dan-Michael

now we fade to black

Tsunamis Within

Ship of Dreams

Takeshi *knew* that it must have been Manuel and Tony who stole the largest squash from his family's vegetable garden. He had seen them hanging around a couple of times, peeking through the wooden fence before picking up groceries at his family's store. It must have been them. But why? What for? Masaharu, Takeshi's father, suspected the same. "It was dose damn Puerto Rican boys," he said. "Had to be dose damn borinkees."

But they had left it at that. In the midst of the booming town of Palama in west Honolulu during a time that immigrants of different backgrounds were finding common ground in their shared plight, it was not good to make waves. No more fights among the workers. Cooperation, instead, was to prevail. Sharing of food, drink, and dreams.

The year was nineteen twenty-two. At nineteen, Takeshi was growing up with the century that had three years on him. It had been a century of mixed blessings, mixed promises thus far. *The* war had ended. The League of Nations would prevent any more. Yet during Takeshi's last year at McKinley High School, his teacher, Mr. Armstrong, often stated that the worst was yet to come. What was happening in Russia, he would say cryptically, would have unprecedented impact on the rest of the world. His classmates — children of the plantations — paid little attention. The world, the century, was theirs to conquer. America, which claimed them as its own, offered unlimited opportunities. Never mind that the glories of the Hawaiian monarchy were dimming, for the legacies of Prince Kuhio and Queen Liliuokalani were torches lit, *malamalama.* More important, the legacy of democracy existed now for the benefit of all. This legacy was being tested

15

by, among other things, the many strikes on plantations by Japanese, Filipinos, and Puerto Ricans . . .

But Takeshi's father had had enough of that. After saving bits of his meager earnings for twenty-odd years, and thanks to *tanomoshi* and a small bank loan, he finally obtained enough capital to quit the plantation and start his own small store.

The family lived in back of the store, though Takeshi had managed to gather enough scrap lumber to build himself a little loft above. He needed *some* privacy, what with four younger brothers and sisters doing what young children do.

Takeshi spent his mornings *hapai*-ing rice in 100-pound burlap bags, stacking potatoes, oranges, yams, stocking shelves with cans of soup and meat, as well as other everyday needs like flour, milk, lard, beans, and shoyu .

He missed going to school. His dream of being a lawyer had left with the ship that brought him and his father their first load of goods at Honolulu Harbor. Whether that ship of dreams would return remained to be seen.

The Puerto Ricans—at least what Takeshi knew of them—were a complicated lot. Boisterous in their manners, relationships, and very much like the Hawaiians in their openness, their sense of family. Yet they were awfully repressed in their Catholicity in a way that Hawaiians—who had converted to all shades of Christianity—were not. While Hawaiian girls were still quite casual about their dress—in the rural areas one would occasionally see women bare-topped and unaffected—Puerto Rican girls appeared intriguingly puritanical in dresses that covered their bodies from their necks on down to the ground they walked on. Takeshi recalled a story told one night when Masaharu and a Japanese friend remembered in their drunken revelry (thanks to some homemade brew) how shocked the Puerto Rican women—some Portuguese women, too—were when the Japanese men paraded down the dirt road in only towels on their way to the *furo*. "Da girls, dey wen' scream," the friend said, "and we nevah know what dey was screaming about!" They roared, falling on the ground in laughing fits. Then, after they finally recovered for brief silent moments of sober reflection one of them came up with another "old times" story that had been told and heard a hundred times before.

Those same Puerto Rican women really loosened up on Saturday nights, however. What Masaharu and others called "kachi-kachi" music thumped from the social hall on School Street where the Puerto Ricans congregated, along with some Portuguese, Hawaiians, a smattering of whites and Filipinos. (The Chinese, Japanese, and Koreans still preferred far eastern means of expressing themselves, like sake and *kachashi*.)

Some of the younger Asian kids, like Takeshi, spent much of their Saturday evenings on one of the mango trees outside the social hall, peering inside, entranced by the goings on. Takeshi would gaze in wild-eyed wonder at these weekend bursts of exuberance — the changa-changa strumming of different sized guitars, the maracas doing things with time that no hourglass would, the joyful if other-worldly singing, and that *da kine, ah, wha-cha-ma-call-it* thing that made the scratchy sound that held it all together, the wild fits of . . . *dancing?* And the drunken fist fights and arguments by men concerning their women that culminated each dream-like Saturday night.

Takeshi was surprised that brisk April evening when he saw his half-drunk father struggling to climb up the tree to join him and some other young boys. He knew he had nothing to fear, though, as the sake seemed to break down the differences between the *issei* and *nisei* males and inspired boy-like camaraderie.

"Dese damn borinkees. Dey no quit, eh?" Masaharu said when he finally reached the limb his son sat on.

"Hey, be careful, Papa. You can fall, you know."

"Me fall?" Masaharu laughed. "Me monkey, you know. Jes' like you." As he said this he slipped and would have fallen if his son had not grabbed him by the shirt with lightning speed.

"I tole you be careful."

Masaharu snickered as Takeshi helped him get safely settled where two branches forked and formed a somewhat comfortable chair. For minutes they silently watched the romp and revelry. Finally Masaharu spoke.

"Dass . . . dass my squash!" he said, pointing into the hall accusingly.

"What?" Takeshi answered. "What'chu talking about?"

Already his father was climbing down the tree, pressing tightly against the tree trunk, seemingly sobered. Takeshi was bewildered. He saw no squash. He swung down the tree and followed his father, who stormed into the hall and through the crowded dance floor till he stood in front of the band, specifically the *jibaro* who relentlessly dictated rhythm with the scratcher.

The music stopped. Takeshi felt the heat of a thousand eyes on him and his crazy father.

"Dass my squash!" he declared, pointing at the scratcher, a finely carved, etched, and painted gourd that any Japanese would normally be appreciative of. The musicians laughed. An old Puerto Rican man, also quite drunk, made his way up front.

"Whasamatta, Masaharu-san?" he said, partly inquisitive, partly annoyed. "Why you come bodda us?"

"You," Masaharu said, recognizing Pablo, a former plantation co-worker. "Yo' sons . . .," he said, getting bug-eyed, "dey wen steal . . . my squash!"

"Manny! Get yo' okole ovah heah right now!" the old man shouted. Takeshi shook his head. He pressed his nose-bridge with his index finger and thumb, shut his eyes for several seconds, thinking *This isn't happening. This isn't happening.* He then opened his eyes to see a well dressed young man emerging from the crowd. "How you get dis *guiro?*" Pablo said, referring to the scratcher.

"No was me, dad. Was Tony dem."

"No lie," a female voice from the crowd said. "Was *you* and Tony, Manny." The accuser emerged from the crowd. Takeshi recognized Manny's sister, Linda. He and Linda had been school chums, a few years back. But he hadn't seen her in school during the last two years.

"*Sinverguenza!*" Pablo slapped his much larger son in the head.

"Was Tony's idea," Manny said, cowering. "He—" The father grabbed him by the frilly sleeve of his shirt.

"No, Pablo," Masaharu said, pleading. "Nevah mind. Let him go."

Pablo didn't hear. He was cursing his son in Spanish, pushing him out toward the door as everyone followed. Takeshi could not help but steal quick glances at Linda. She was beautiful now, he thought. The full breasts, the color on her cheeks. Half the crowd, Takeshi and his father included, followed Pablo and Manny out of the hall. By then Pablo had removed his belt and

was yelling, "Wheah's Tony? Wheah da hell is dat damn kid?"
Pablo was still deaf to Masaharu's pleas of "Nevah mind, nevah
mind," as he led his son up the dirt road and into the darkness.

The crowd went in.

The music went on.

Takeshi was back on the tree when Masaharu finally returned
from wherever he had disappeared to and again was struggling to
climb up. Takeshi hadn't noticed his father climbing up the tree.
His ears were attuned to the music, but his eyes were too focused to be
enjoying the generalities of the partying and scuffling. He seemed
captivated. What Masaharu saw in his son's eyes was not the stare
of mere enchantment. One look and he knew his son was more
lost than anyone he ever knew had ever been in this crazy sugar
and pineapple paradise.

Takeshi was stricken by *love.*

Masaharu peered into the hall from his roost, squinting his
Japanese eyes till he too noticed the radiance. *Must be the one
that glows.* Masaharu slapped his son's head. "Go home! Now!
Hayaku!"

Takeshi, jarred out of his dream world, sadly swung on an
outhanging branch, his feet just barely reaching yet landing on
another branch in a way only one brought up around trees could.
Simultaneously, his knees collapsed as his hands grasped that same
branch and the movement was repeated. He then made a short
drop, feet first, to the ground. Again his father struggled down,
sliding down the trunk, arms and legs wrapped tightly and still
he fell on his ass.

Masaharu got up and again slapped his son on the head muttering "*Bakatare* . . . stoopid boy . . . stoo-pid boy. Mo' bettah
send back Japan. . . ."

That night in bed Takeshi closed his eyes to clearly see Linda's
face, the way she dimpled when she smiled. He imagined touching
her large breasts, unraveling her braided hair. He pretended, as
best he could, that he was having sex with her. For as long as he
could handle it. Finally, with the vague image of her thighs no
longer pounding through his head, and after having felt simultaneously the ecstacy and pain of his wild imagination and fruitless
dreams, Takeshi fell asleep on the wet spot, snoring snores as long

in time as the stroke of a rough-hewn stick across a shining gourd.

The cock crowed. It was four a.m. Takeshi groaned. Then he remembered it was Sunday. He would get two whole hours more of sleep. He thanked God for resting that day so he could too, and hummed himself back to sleep.

Takeshi was pulling weeds in the family garden that afternoon when she came.

"Ah, excuse me," she said.

That voice. "Wha'?" Takeshi muttered as he looked up and saw Linda standing over him carrying a package. He had no shirt on, no footwear, only an old pair of khakis rolled up to knee length. He was suddenly very aware of his appearance.

She blushed, the color of cinnamon. She wore a *kinuli* shirt and faded denim overalls, her hair in two pigtail braids. She took something out of the package. "Dis fo' your faddah." It was the gourd in its new state, an explicit and implicit piece of art. "And dis fo' your family. Ah, um. Spanish rice with gandule beans. . . . My faddah said he real sorry about what da boys did."

"Nah . . . 'ass okay. No problem." Takeshi managed to say as he tried to grab the gourd and package without making contact with the girl of his most recent dream. Still, the back of his left hand brushed against her left breast in the exchange. She smiled. He blushed. "Ah . . . tanks. But you guys should've kept dis . . . ah . . ."

"Oh, you dunno my fadda . . ."

"Well . . . tanks." He felt more nervous each second. "Ah . . . you wen change school?"

"No," she said frankly. 'I had to quit . . . I heard you wen' graduate." Takeshi nodded. "Too good. . . . Well, I bettah go." Linda started to leave.

"How come you wen' quit?" She turned toward him and shrugged her shoulders.

"You should come to da dance Saturday night," she said suddenly, then turned and began walking away. There was an inch-wide hole in her pants that revealed some flesh.

Wait. I love you, he wanted to cry out. But he kept his mouth shut. She must have a dozen suitors, he thought. And I'm

20

Japanese. It would be easier to climb Mount Fuji *hadashi* than to get permission from mama and papa. Especially papa. And what about *her* parents? They might have already arranged a marriage for her.

Takeshi did not know the customs of Puerto Ricans, how they went about such things. But he understood one thing, one thing that cut through all beliefs and customs: What he felt had to be dealt with. He could not keep his feelings hidden for long. He felt as if love had carved its way into his chest, and his entire being trembled from the feeling. He got chicken skin. With his free hand he rubbed his opposite arm hard to soothe the myriad bumps. He gazed at the gourd. The care that had gone into shaping the wood — the perfectly aligned grooves — and then painting in the achote-red lines like Indian warpaint was almost — almost Japanese. If he could look that good in her eyes . . .

That night Takeshi dreamt about the guiro. He had taken it with him out to the southern side of Sand Island and placed it, hole side up, with stick inside, into the ocean. He gently pushed it away. It returned. He pushed it away, again. Again it returned, this time altered. Each time he pushed it away, it returned in a slightly different form: a double-hulled canoe, a schooner, a steamer. . . . Then he noticed that an old Hawaiian woman, dressed in a *kikepa,* stood behind him and off to the side. She wore a faint smile, and shook her head slowly. He shuddered. The last time a wave brought it in, Takeshi noticed a piece of paper inside. He quickly took it out of the Chinese junk that it now resembled.

The paper was blank.

The message was clear.

The image of Linda walking away in her puka overalls stayed with him for days. During those same days Takeshi — stomach warmed by miso — sailed through the morning routine that began with daybreak at the docks with its oranges and blues, unloading crates that were to stock empty shelves, mulching, weeding, and *hanawai*-ing the garden, gathering the ready vegetables, nurturing the sizable squashes his father proudly grew, always noticing the broken vine where the stolen one had been, secretly proud of his new plaything, practicing on it every chance he could.

He took the gourd on his afternoon journeys up the Kapalama

21

Stream. His escape. *Scrrape, chuk-chuk. Scrrape, chuk-chuk.* He became obsessed with trying to capture the rhythm. Playing out his dream, he placed the gourd in the water. It did not return. Instead it was quickly swept downstream. Takeshi chased it alongside the bank, dashing like a mongoose through the thicket, and finally dived, fully clothed, to capture it.

He laughed like a child.

Masaharu had not believed his son when Takeshi had told him about what he had done that Saturday night. Takeshi showed him the guiro as evidence. Masaharu reacted by staying sober all week, trying to remember. Takeshi knew his father had finally pieced together the events when Masaharu began telling his son, over and over. *Japanese girl good fo' you. Odda kine girl, no good.*

Takeshi was restless in bed all that week. Sometimes he carried 100-pound bags in his sleep, stacking them head high. He would wake up and remind himself that work was pau. *Pau* hana, he told himself. Rest time. He tried to think of other things. Like Linda. A future.

The mango wars didn't help. That was what Takeshi called the season's first falling of mango on the Quonset roofs. BOOM! WHABAM! It sounded like another World War.

The night moans of his parents from the next room did not help either. Was that his destiny? To moan at night from the aches of too many years of long hours of backbreaking work?

Saturday came. Mr. Armstrong walked into the store. Takeshi had been sitting behind the jars of pickled plum and dried fruit practicing his stroke on the guiro.

"So this is the family store," Mr. Armstrong said.

"Yeah. Dis is it," Takeshi said. They shook hands.

"Say, this is a strange looking calabash." Mr. Armstrong had noticed the carved gourd. Takeshi handed it over to him.

"Nice, yeah?"

"Very nice." Mr. Armstrong held the gourd up. "This is the baby form of Lono, the god of fertility, agriculture, music . . . everything nice."

"Wha'chu talking about?"

"Lono. The Hawaiian god who oversees the Makahiki festivities." He looked at his former student, stating matter-of-factly,

22

"You don't know that?" Takeshi shrugged his shoulders. "This is the very stuff the schools ought to be teaching, the meaningful stuff."

"Hey, ah . . ." Takeshi said. "But dass Puerto Rican. Not Hawaiian."

"Hmmmm . . . I *knew* there was something different about this. Different yet same. Nice." He handed the gourd back to Takeshi. "Well, I better get what I came for." Mr. Armstrong began gathering groceries. Afterwards he and Takeshi talked a bit more, about Takeshi's fellow McKinley graduates who spent their days diving for coins dropped from passenger ships like the *Lurline* at Pier 10, about those who were *furyoshonin,* pool hall bums, about the general lack of opportunities for non-whites, especially Orientals, who were seen by the white oligarchy as a threat. Before he left, Mr. Armstrong, as if he were again lecturing Takeshi in a class, as if he could read his former student's mind, stated, "You know, I've missed so many boats in my lifetime, I thought I'd never get anywhere. But look now, I'm here. All the way from New York. And, believe me, this is paradise. No matter what anybody says . . . I guess what I'm trying to say is that another boat will always come. See you later." He left.

Takeshi was carrying the guiro—which was tied on a string to his left hand—that night when he climbed the mango tree outside the social hall. It was nine o'clock and the place was starting to explode. Those who drank were drunk by now. Two fist fights had started out of the blue and had ended in a manner even more vague. The guitarists—playing guitars of all sizes—strummed harder and harder, shouting out their Spanish words to be heard above the din. And the poor guiro player—playing a gourd half the size of the one Takeshi carried—struggled to keep up with the demands for increased volume. Takeshi, numbed observer of all the madness, could not resist the temptation to start scraping his own guiro from his unique position. At first he played softly, not even attracting the attention of those around him. But then he too got lost in the rhythm and before Manny made him realize it, had begun to dictate it from afar.

"Ay! Get yo' ass down here, Japanee." The voice was Manny's. Takeshi was hesitant but saw the futility of not complying. He silently cursed his father for not passing on to him his knowledge of *jujitsu* and, holding the gourd in one hand and the stick in his mouth, made the easy jump down. Takeshi had seen enough Saturday night scrapes to be pretty sure he would be involved in the next one.

"Ay," said Manny, leaning quite a bit and grinning wide. "If you like play da music, you go *in*side. Not out here. Come on." Manny grabbed Takeshi by the arm.

"No," Takeshi said, pulling back. "Ass okay. I no like."

"Come on. No be shame! We all da same, ovah here. No be shame," Manny repeated. "Everybody too drunk fo' notice anyway." Takeshi found himself being pulled into the hall and to the front in mid-song. Manny urged him on, pantomiming the art of guiro playing and shouting, "Toca! Toca, Japonesa!"

Takeshi finally succumbed to the strong will of Manny, playing softly, with hesitation. Smiles from the band, some familiar faces, comforted him. Shame gave way to relief.

"Da feel!" one band member shouted. "Yeah. You get da feeling, my friend."

"Welcome aboard!" another shouted as Takeshi slipped onto the stage.

Takeshi knew he had broken through some godawful barrier — within himself. He couldn't help but smile at the thought that was forming, the thought of being the helmsman of the ship that would sail on through the night, through the sea of dancers, across the ocean of lost opportunities. . . . He just wanted to steer her right.

Then there was Linda. Takeshi spotted her (it wasn't hard), her eyes shining like beacons in the darkness, her unbraided hair flowing in waves about her shoulders, dancing to the rhythms, and her smile . . . When Linda spotted him, she winked him on, snapping her fingers like castanets.

24

Clear Acrylic Enamel

Now it comes. Clear Acrylic Enamel. Funny how it hits you
long after you've given up trying to remember. Boy, it had a
good taste. Wouldn't even bother to describe it. Like sex, acid,
death, and adulthood, you gotta try it to know what it's about.
I let the feeling capture me. It had long been reverberating in the
inner recesses of my mind and now something—a smell, a taste,
a sound—has summoned it to the forefront, ringing clear, to be
absorbed NOW! before it is reduced to fragmented memories.

Silver lips. It is my memory now. Our insides must have
primed, lacquered and enameled. I wonder if the paint eroded
any in the past two years.

Lenny is trying to sneak in. Arthur's verbally seducing two
chicks. Me? I'm watching. I've been watching since sixty-nine
when my fingers were slammed by a yardstick and my terrified
eyes watched her mouth moving "In my class you pay attention!"
The mean, craggy, Oriental face. I had merely been leaning back
on the two rear legs of my chair against the wall, with one ear
pressed against it, trying to hear what went on on the other side.
No. It must have been the paint. Sharpened me insenses or some-
think. Made life a motion picture, an Edward Hopper painting
come to life, with me, Lenny and Arthur the central characters,
the subjects.

These nights were a movie. The same movie again and again,
weekend after weekend, concert after concert—sneaking in.
It's become a habit, me, Lenny and Arthur sneaking into concerts.
HIC Arena, Waikiki Shell, Andrews Amphitheater. Wherever
concerts were held, the film was being done on location. It was
always challenging enough not to get boring, like the pinball

machines at Rainbow Billiards, when we mastered them to the point that the games weren't fun anymore.

Sneaking in is hard. Well, not so much at Andrews, with its not-too-high chain-link fence, its relatively easy to climb walls. One could even go under the fence at one part, while the less risky (LRs) climbed one of the portable buildings around the amphitheater for the loftier view.

Getting into the Waikiki Shell is difficult. The fence is higher than that of Andrews. Once you get over the fence at most of the points around the place, you have to run across a field and hurdle still another fence (if you are able to avoid being tackled by a cop who is just itching (and I mean itching) to rough you up). The best chance is to leap the fence by the bathroom, run into it and calmly take a piss.

HIC Arena? Now that's a brand-new ballgame. Those of you with weak hearts better go and buy tickets right now, if any are left. It's a flying-saucer-(modern, I guess) shaped castle, complete with a moat around it. No alligators, though, just millions of tilapia, not to mention a sizable number of ducks. The best possible way of getting in without the ticket that lets you cross the drawbridge is to creep along the walls which have a fairly long footwide ledge, leap a waist-high railing, dart toward the stairs and either sit down conspicuously on the stairs if there are no empty seats or walk around all night like you're spaced out. The only problem is getting over that little railing without being grabbed by a cop or security officer who usually is waiting to knock you into the moat.

The cop — male, about thirty, local — is waiting for Lenny, who is standing along a ledge with his back against the wall. The cop senses he is there though he can't see Lenny because the ledge he is on projects like an *L*. The cop is at the top point of the letter and Lenny is balancing along at the bottom. It is only when Lenny turns the corner that the police officer can see who is crazy enough to make the attempt. I wipe my forehead, signaling Lenny that the cop is present. He retreats to the diagonally-opposite end of the top of the L-shaped wall and onto the safety of the grass.

It's important to me that Lenny gets in — I don't care if I can't do it and Arthur's more into scoring with chicks anyway —

because Lenny's the best. Sneaky, clever, and gusty as hell. What's more—dig it—he's on a streak. He's gotten in free eighteen times in a row, man. Not the last eighteen concerts (who wants to see the Carpenters?), but eighteen times in eighteen. He's *got* to get in. Our goal is twenty. That's why I'm standing here on the grass giving him signals. You follow me? Maybe there's paint in you. Remember, movies don't provide you with instant replays like T.V. does. And sometimes you have to read the book first.

The cop moves from his position and stands by the snack bar which is contained within the L-shaped wall. He is itching to bust Lenny's or any non-payer's (NP) head. There is and isn't a crowd outside. No cohesion. Not like that Hendrix concert when Lance was still around and before I began watching, when some weird sonofabitch pulls a fifth column by accidentally (hmmm) leaning on the wide bar that disengaged the lock on these side doors, doors flying open, with fifty bodies smashing through. Then, with the security officers (SO) chasing them all over the place and the notoriously-innocent guy yelling "Wha'd I do? Wha'd I do?" me, Lenny, Arthur, Lance and some other guys who later changed into Double Knit Assholes (DNA) are sucked in by the wide vaccum and settle on the steps inside just in time to hear Hendrix make the "Star-Spangled Banner" worth listening to, shortly before he was shot. Wait. Wait. It was King who was shot. Christ, I'm getting history distorted. I don't know who was murdered, who simply OD'd and who was watching as I am now.

Maybe that's what I'm doing: Seeing that history comes out straight and clear—truth in other words—because I know now that Lenny, who approaches me now, is making history.

"Pretty rough tonight," I say.
"Ah, fuck, we get 'em. Even if I gotta swim." His words make me look at the ducks for some reason. "Where Atta went?"
"Where else?" I turn my head toward Arthur and the two girls, and point with my index finger.
"The fuckah," he says. Lenny, with his hands in his pocket—as if to make his shoulders look bigger—approaches Arthur who is conversing with a couple of Oriental girls. Both Lenny and Arthur are the same height, about five-eight, but Lenny's features

are obviously Filipino while Arthur's reveal some Hawaiian. I have never asked him what the rest is. Me? I'm watching. Not only watching, but following Lenny so I can also listen. I see that Lenny, perhaps instinctively, approaches the shorter of the two girls.

"Hey, you like fuck?" One thing about Lenny, he's honest. The girl turns color before my eyes, different shades of red. "Man, I know you like fuck." Color Arthur steaming purple, the other girl pale.

"We better go da odda side," the taller girl says. The two girls walk away. Arthur turns to Lenny. He is angry but doesn't want to speak too loud.

"You fuckah!" he says. "What you trying? I had the fuckah! Shit. Now I gotta start all ovah again."

Lenny glares back at him. "Shit. We no mo' all night! Man, if they like, they like! Why waste our fucking time? You like get in or not!"

"Fuck the concert!" Arthur yells. "I rather get laid!" For some strange reason, whenever they start to argue they glance toward me as if I should say something.

"Clear Acrylic Enamel." What else could I say?

"Hey, yeah!" Arthur says, "Thass the one!" Lenny does not look enthused, because he is. His facial expressions are incredibly downplayed, like the expressions of someone who knows there's a camera on him and wishes to deceive it.

"Thass the baby," Lenny says. "Taste so fucking sweet, man." Lenny's tone changes suddenly, addressing me. "Hey, you goin' try or what? This fuckah," he points to Arthur, "he retire already."

"I goin' try," I say. "But you gotta get in first."

"No make difference. I can get in by myself."

"Sure, Lenny," Arthur interjects. "Sure." Within a few minutes we agree that Lenny has to get in first. We try the same place with me and Arthur playing first and third base coach, respectively. It is too risky and we stop him before he gets thrown out. We decide to wait until intermission.

Minutes later the crowd starts pouring out of the inner sanctum. It is intermission.

You may leave now. Be back in about ten minutes.
What? You're still here? Intermissions can be important, too?

28

Really?

The inside crowd is not a crowd. No cohesion. Faces are
not faces. I see glazed eyes, eyelids painted blue, green, eyes
drifting, eyebrows lifting, lids sagging, eyes passing eyes, ass
grabbing eyes. But the clothes! Polyester, double-knit slacks, hip-
hugging perma-press jeans, skimpy blouses, perma-wrinkled silks
shirts, sandals, slippers, high-heeled shoes, all suggesting that the
music is of secondary importance. One can always tell who's playing by the crowd. Most of the people wander around, captured in
a web of paranoic tranquility. A few stand by the railing that
keeps them from falling into the moat and stare, outward, at us.
Actually, a lot of them are staring at the ducks.
        The ducks! Why didn't I think of that?
        "Lenny. Atta." I sound enthused. "We go give them one
dee-coy." Arthur looks puzzled, while Lenny, though he may be
puzzled, seems to have it figured out already. I tell Arthur to go
along the *L* ledge and attract attention. Not too obviously, though.
Lenny has already figured out his part. He heads toward another
ledge about ninety feet to the left of the L-shaped one.
        People on the outside see Arthur on the ledge and watch
me play third-base coach, a job I relish. They seem to be united
by this valiant effort. The cop, sensing something, acts like
nothing is going on. He doesn't want to stop the attempt, but
rather wipe out whoever reaches the railing. Those standing at
the railing sense what's happening too. They're actually paying
attention.
        Arthur is all smiles. The cop *knows* I'm giving signals and
pretends otherwise. Then, this lady security officer, twentyish,
slightly overweight, who's been guarding the ledge ninety feet
to the left senses that something's up and unobtrusively walks in
the direction of the cop. Lenny steals across the ledge like no one
else can, leaps the unguarded railing and is lost in the inside
crowd. Number nineteen. One more to go. The outside crowd
applauds. Arthur sticks his head around the corner of the
L-shaped wall and smiles at the puzzled cop and equally puzzled
security lady. Intermission is over.

After seeing the inside crowd and sensing that the cop is

itching to get me, I don't try very hard to get in. I end up
joining Arthur, who is now talking to the taller of the two chicks.
I start talking to the other one, and me and Arthur end up
heading toward the car with the two faceless girls.

The morning after, while me and Arthur are blessed with
aching balls, Lenny is telling us how great a concert it wasn't.
A wasted effort.

"Yeah, Lenny, yeah," me and Arthur harmonize.

"Fucking teasers," Arthur adds, "wasting my fucking dope."

"*Our* fucking dope," Lenny says.

"That's the trip," I say. "Painted eyelids are for teasing, Clear
Acrylic does the pleasing." I do not know what the fuck I am talking about which is cool because none of us do most of the time.
It is this absurdity that links us together. Words, by necessity,
take on different shades of meaning in the continuously evolving
process of language. We understand the absurdity; that's what
matters. My words sent their minds back in time (Or did their
minds summon a piece of their past? What goes where?) Anyway,
we reminisce.

We live in a two-bedroom apartment in Makiki, the low-
rise, apartment/condominium center of the Pacific that lies in the
shadow of Punchbowl, the extinct crater now used as a national
cemetery. The three of us sleep in the bedroom with wall-to-wall
mattresses and floor to ceiling naked lady posters and assorted
scrawls and drawings. In the other room we keep our guitars
and assorted instruments — harmonicas, tambourines, maracas,
parts of a drum set, and an old honky-tonk piano. We just play
for fun now since Lance, our lead singer, is away. The combination
living room/kitchen has only the essentials: a gas stove, a small
refrigerator and a sink (of course) on one end; a foot high table in
mid-center with *gozas* under and around it, which we now sit on;
a telephone on the wall that bisects the apartment; and, against
that same wall, a *Pioneer* stereo component system replete with
the kind of speakers that make neighbors complain.

It had taken us about a year to fix the rust on our '64 Volkswagen. It belongs to me, Lenny, Arthur and Lance, should he
return. That's how we got into the paint thing. Yesterday, Saturday, we sanded down all the rusty areas and patched up the holes

with *Bondo*. Then we sprayed those areas with a primer. The scent sent us into our pre-car adolescent sniffing days, the pre-grass phase. Then, like right now, we reminisced on our spacing out, on our hearing the "Now I *know* I'm stoned!" buzz, and, unforgettably, we laughed over the time we didn't use the usual colorless acrylic paint and stood out at a dance-party because our silver lips glowed in the dark. Silver lips, the more we thought of it the more we laughed. It was the accidental yet obvious emblem of our defiance. Our own silly way of saying *fuck your world.*

But we couldn't figure out what paint gave us the best high until I flashed on it last night at the concert.

Sundays are dull, duller when it's cloudy. And they are dullest when it is early November and clouds are a sign of what's to come. Makes you almost wanna put on your Sunday best and go to church, just for the hell of it. I am on the verge of putting on something decent when Lenny suggests we go to Sandy Beach.

"If we goin' get wet, we might as well get drenched," he says. The day might be salvaged. The only problem is who is willing to drive. It's always a struggle.

"My leg sore," Arthur says, getting off to a good start, holding his left nut for emphasis.

"Fuck," Lenny says, "My eyes too fucking phased out, man."

"I'll drive," I mumble.

"Shit, my leg!" Arthur squeezes tighter.

"You only need one leg, pal," Lenny says.

"What about the fucking clutch?" Arthur counters.

"Shove it up your fucking nose," Lenny says, smiling.

"I'll drive," I say louder. They continue to argue for a full minute before they realize I have offered to drive, to everyone's surprise, including mine. "But everybody gotta chip in fo' gas."

It is a thirty-five minute drive to Sandy Beach from our apartment in Makiki, in the midst of the mess that is Honolulu, but if we're lucky we'll make it in an hour. First we stop for gas at the service station where we work. Then we head toward an on-ramp to the H-1 Freeway. All the car windows are open because the overhanging clouds and the tall buildings on each side of the narrow street box us in enough already. When we are on the freeway we breathe easier as this stretch of freeway on the way to Sandy Beach rises high above the city.

Honolulu is like a woman who doesn't know what she's got and does everything to look more like someone else every passing day, the someone else being L.A.

They've shaven your pubic palm trees
and replaced them with a concrete slab . . .
Out of which grow sky high cement stubbles that
make you look so drab . . .
. . . Oh, no, Lulu, what have they done to you.

Nobody's singing. And the words aren't mine. Words from a song Lance wrote echo in my mind. I then flash on the last, unfinished lyric he showed me:

When you look at the world through high-priced cameras
there's an even higher price you have to pay
I'm sorry what you see is not more glamorous a snapshot
you want orange, you're only getting gray . . .
Take off the lens cap, take in the landscape
stay away from the mind traps that people call "escape"
Be sure it's not another trap that you're escaping to
and just as negatives develop, so will you . . .

"Hey," Lenny says from behind me. "You sleeping o' what?"

"No," I answer, snapping out of the daze induced by the highway, "just meditating my ass off."

"I just wanted to make sure you know wha's happenin' ahead."

"Yeah." We have come to the part where the freeway ceases to be a freeway and becomes a highway, with traffic lights and all.

As we cruise down the long stretch of road known as Kalanianaole Highway, most of the claustrophobia is gone. No tall buildings. Just good old suburban-type homes, wide streets and all. Everyone knows that the wider the streets are, the nicer the homes. Quite unlike the one-lane two-way streets in Palama . . . Whoops. Starting to daydream again. Better keep my eyes on the road. In other words watch.

Trees are abundant on both sides of the highway, swaying slightly in a gentle breeze that is not so gentle for us as we now fly down the road. Lenny tells me to stop at Koko Marina Shopping Center a little further up.

I turn in to the parking area of the shopping center and park alongside a curb, because parking's hard to find and me and Arthur will wait in the car anyway. Lenny dashes out. I turn up the car radio:

> *"There must be some kinda way outa here,"*
> *said the joker to the thief.*
> *"There's too much confusion,*
> *I can't get no relief. . . ."*

"Hendrix sings the shit outa that song," Arthur says. I nod.
It starts to drizzle. Lenny returns in a couple of minutes with a
package. Arthur asks him what he bought. Lenny says "Dig!"
when I turn back onto the highway, I am in the right-most lane.
Arthur tells me to shift into the next lane because the one we're in
feeds into it up ahead.

With the drizzle, with my mind into Hendrix's frenzied guitar-
work, and his rendering of Dylan's words: "There are many here
among us who feel that life is but a joke," and with my eyes
checking the side mirror for cars and my hands turning the wheel
simultaneously, by the time my awareness is set on what's ahead
by Arthur's "Hey!" I find myself running a red light. I blast my
horn without knowing why. Perhaps it's an instinctive grasp for
legitimacy. The other guys laugh and wave at the cars we pass.
As we head uphill, I gaze into the rear-view mirror for a cop's
flashing blue light but only see the two red traffic lights. As the
lights get fainter, I am increasingly relieved, secure as the drizzle
stops and splinters of sunlight penetrate the clouds.

We arrive at the beach. Somehow water lures us like nothing
else, with the possible exception of music. Arthur passes by two
chicks on beach towels — straining to maintain their tans, I guess
— with scarcely a glance. He wants to bodysurf as much as me and
Lenny do. I guess his balls still ache and he knows the therapeutic
value of a whirlpool of salt water.

Lenny and Arthur are pros in the ocean. They carve through
waves, weave under them, slice the fucking ocean to ribbons.
Me, I get smashed. But don't get me wrong. I love every fucking
shorebreak of wave that smashes me into the sand. I love when it
sucks me in for more, and thrashes me again because I know I'll
somehow manage to sneak in a couple of good rides.

It's funny how we take to the ocean after Lance's disap-
pearance. The papers say he drowned. I don't believe what I read.
They never found the body. I dive under a mother of a wave.
Lance split. Me, Lenny and Arthur know that. It was the first and

last time I dropped acid. The four of us were walking along the sea wall at Ala Moana when the acid hit. I am drifting now. At that instant we transformed into the Beatles walking down Abbey Road. I felt I was part of an album cover. Who could imagine how they felt, how me, Lenny and Arthur felt when it started to become a four-way street, when Lance broke toward the beach, dove into the water, and swam toward the crooked bowl of moon as water slowly filled it. All we saw afterwards, when we swam out there, was a blinking red light. We spent the whole night looking for him, long after the rescue unit gave up. I am drifting out more. He didn't know how to drown. Besides, he had plans. We don't talk about Lance much — his quiet, calculated movements that almost obscured his constant agitation — but we knew better than to go to a fucking memorial service. I tread water. He was weird but he was the sharpest of us. His conception of the world was getting people to sneak *out* of concerts. Damn it. He's just playing some super sly game, waiting for the right time. He's gone under — *yughh,* so have I. I've swallowed a mouthful. What a taste.

It sometimes takes hours to describe a moment. On the other hand . . . Hours later I fall down on the wet sand. I look up ahead and see Lenny ripping his towel apart.

There's a buzzing in my head. Someone is watching me. In fact there's a lot of them. I stare up from behind the sea wall. No choice. I make a run for it into the ethereal darkness. I stumble, scraping the tops of my toes. My mind runs back to a Santana concert at the Shell. There's at least a thousand of us outside. We have two things in common: we hate (or can't afford) to pay for music, and we want to get in. The vast majority of us are male. More than half are white guys, *haoles.* There are no fences between them and us shaded folks. There's a proliferation of attempts to get inside. Cops slam the ones they catch against the fence, then make them climb back out. Some return bleeding. Twenty police cars are parked at one end of Kapiolani Park, which partially surrounds the Shell. A couple of cops are giving tickets to cars parked along a dirt road in another part of the park. Cops on motorcycles drive through the crowd, dispersing us, as we get rowdier by the minute. The cops get even rowdier and force us

34

to dive out of the way. Santana starts to play. The percussionistic spray of beat captures something in us, something wildly primitive. Some crazy fucker climbs the fence. Then another . . . and another . . . then a hundred. I start to climb as the screaming guitar pierces the wall of fear. Halfway on top I stop because I don't see Lance, Lenny, and Arthur. No! I stop because there's more going on outside! I leap back. Lance runs up to me with a bunch of parking tickets he pulled off the windshields of cars. The police department is gonna have one hell of a time convincing people that they got tickets tonight.

The buzzing gets louder. We drift from Abbey Road and float through a world of dark, only starlit space and metronomic, undulating rhythm. Secrets unfold as universes open like sleepy eyes. Seemingly impenetrable boundaries unbound, reveal themselves as clear walls of sound, soaking in an ocean of black, spacy void. Space. Rhythm. Space. Rhythm. The HIC Arena floats by. In the starlight of distance far beyond, I see Lance . . . filming it all. A silver circle is spinning, I am finding. Unwinding. Unwind.

I am staring at the door latch release button of the Volkswagen. I no longer hear the buzz. I see a piece of towel in my hand and realize it is dark. We are still at the beach, for christ's sake! Hypnotized by a fucking release button?

I am freezing my ass as I get up to look for Lenny and Arthur. I am headed toward the bathroom when I see them walking along the beach with rags held to their mouths. I see a blinding flash right at Lenny's waist. It is the moon's reflection off a paint can, partially tucked in his shorts.

Monday. Arthur has managed to get the phone number of the girl he met at last Saturday's concert by calling up all the "Wongs" at random in the phone book. I laughed everytime he said "Wong numbah" and slammed the phone. He tries to make a date for Friday's concert at Andrews. She won't go unless her friend can come along. He tries to get me to take the other girl.

"Come on, you fuckah," he says, cupping the receiver. "I desperate, man."

"No way."

"Hey, come on. I really dig this chick, man. She all right."

"Find some other flower." He tells her he'll call her back later and hangs up the phone. He is quiet for awhile.

"Hey. How about if I pay for your ticket," he says, breaking the silence. He *is* desperate.

"I getting in free," I say, "along with Lenny's record-breaking shot."

"Fuck. He can get in by himself. He not one baby." He is silent for a moment. "Hey, come on. I know we can get us some fucking righteous lays."

"Later." I sense a wall forming. He's pretty pissed off at me, like he is several times a month. This time more so.

It's ten in the morning. Lenny started working at eight. Me and Arthur start working at eleven. We all work as service station attendants at the same place, Herb's Union (HU), in Makiki. I am getting ready to go to work. Arthur's on the phone again.

At work, we talk about the previous day and night and swear never to get nostalgic for a can of paint again, especially one that doesn't give us silver lips.

The week goes by fast. I anxiously await Friday's concert, which features local rather than mainland groups. Arthur is ecstatic to the point of actually being nice to us. The girl finally agreed to go with him to the concert alone. It bothers me and Lenny. We sense that he is one of the DNAs now. Me and Lenny have not discussed the matter but there is no need to. When you go through some profound changes with someone your wave lengths are generally on the same frequency. We know that only Lance's return could knock some sense into Arthur.

I spend my spare time (when I'm alone and it's quiet) drawing. I use the foot-high table for support. I try all kinds of styles, starting with straight forward, representational sketches, then moving toward the abstract utilizing my vague notions of cubism. Now I try to draw a map of Honolulu centering on three points, representing the HIC Arena (to the left of center), the Waikiki Shell (far to the right), and Andrews Amphitheater (above the center). I draw lines connecting them, then a pool-ball rack around them. Then I fill in other places, drawing more and more lines until the paper is a mess. I end up drawing conclusions:

This is fiction, not real. A sound is echoed. It reverberates, is endlessly distorted. Do you see yourself in these lines?

Andrews is quite a place; compact in size, as compared to the other arenas. Its situation in the center of the University of Hawaii guarantees a student audience. Portable buildings linger off two sides of the 'Amphitheater and their rooftops give far better views of concerts than a fairly large arena would. It isn't that difficult to climb the portable buildings either. Just balance yourself on the railing as I am doing now, reach for the roof, then pull yourself up, hugging the roof as if your life depended on it.

While I am struggling to get the greater portion of my body on the roof (being that most of me is dangling), one of the LRs pulls me up and I temporarily join their ranks. As I gaze inside while taking hits from the joints that keep coming to me, I recall the hardness of the concrete seats that circle around the crater-shaped amphitheater and the contrasting softness of the grass in the center, in front of the stage. The majority of the people inside huddle closely on the grass. The ones with meaty asses sit on the concrete, while some bony-assed freaks walk around. I see quadro-fiends, *stereo*ids, lunatics, professors, but no Arthur. I guess he's just a part of the crowd. I decide to go down and join Lenny as, simultaneously, the red spotlight shines from its position on the grass, reflects on the polished steel of a guitar, stabbing my eyes, and the too-loudly-amplified instrument screams in agony. I almost fall off the roof.

I join Lenny outside a side gate, a position that allows for a partial view of the stage. "Lenny, pain is in my ears and in my eyes," I practically sing. I watch the stage act, remembering how a very nervous Lance once told me that each stage is a world.

Sneaking in seems so easy here. The fence-bordered hemisphere leads to a jungle of plants, an ideal place for balling if you don't mind bugs crawling up your ass. The other hemisphere is wall, with a railing on top so no one falls out. If you can race up the wall and into the crowd you're good—or nobody's watching. (Remember, Lenny's the best—and I'm watching.) The security here are not cops, usually, but guys hired by the promoter depending on the promoter's whims. Usually they're university dudes (DUDES) who've got the "ins" with the promoter or his brother. All in all, it looks like number twenty's gonna be no trouble for Lenny, who is biding his time right now.

It's hard to believe the same group is playing. The volume has been toned down and the sound is pleasing to the ear. The music permeates the atmosphere with a folk-rock haze. I stand soaking in the juxtaposition of a stirring bass and drum counterpoint and a high-pitched, intricately woven harmony. I recognize the song to be a Jackson Browne tune as I tune in to the words:

> ... *I thought that I was free but I'm*
> *just one more prisoner of time,*
> *alone within the boundaries of my mind ...*

There is a short instrumental break.

> ... *I thought I was ...*

Delicately piercing three-part harmony. Cut. One voice:

> ... *A child.*

When the music's good who cares about anything else. I actually smile. The cool November air fills my lungs. Good fucking hit.

"I just wen' give it to one of yo' friends," a rowdy voice says, disrupting the acoustic blend. My first thought is to respond. Then I realize that the voice is addressing a haole guy a few feet to my right (Lenny's on my left). The haole guy looks at the source of the voice and says nothing. The source is a husky, Hawaiian-looking guy, carrying a gleaming silver object. It is a flashlight. There are a few other husky guys around him.

The promoter of tonight's concert has a mean streak.

"I talking to you, you fuckah." The husky guy's voice is not rowdy now. It is outright hostility. "I wen' give yo' friend one good whack with dis," he says, waving the flashlight. "I t'ink da bugga stay bleeding. Why you no look?" The haole guy says nothing, doesn't move. "He t'ink he can sneak ovah da fence, eh? I like see you try, you fucking haole."

The last words sting. The connection is clear now. What he is really saying is "I hit one of yours." Does this Hawaiian think of himself as "one of ours"?

My face is on fire. When I turn to look at Lenny's the glow in his eyes suggest the same. There are god knows how many of them. I stand immobile. Me and Lenny, the husky security men, and the two (an unsuspecting fool comes by) haoles form a curious triangle. Three sides rather than three angles. The inside of the triangle is solid, though invisible. We are the edges of clear acrylic walls. There is no straight route to any one of the other sides. Rather, one had to hit his outer edges and make a radical turn. There isn't time and space for that, especially when each side seems to rest on a different plane.

Who created these walls? Were they there all the time?

Moments fail to pass. I close my eyes to prevent their glow from being caught by the gleaming flashlight. I see it shining at me as I provoke assault with taunts: "What you doing in prison, brah? What you doing *inside?*"

The gate swings open and about ten of them charge me, Lenny and any haoles that are nearby. I swing wildly, seeing blood gush from cut eyelids, broken noses, seeing blood on oncoming fists. I see the flashlight coming towards my head. My hands are beaten numb. I can no longer defend myself. I see it all even though nothing has happened. I've just reopened my eyes. Everyone is still on their edge of their triangle side.

You see, I read the book. Does the movie, or should I say silver screen extravaganza, with a cast of god knows how many, end the same way? I turn to Lenny.

'You know what Lance would do in this situation," I say to him.

"Lance is dead!" Lenny screams. "The fuckah is dead!" He runs up to the gate and starts pulling on it. I am frozen.

"Hey, what you trying?" the husky Hawaiian says. "I no like hit you."

Still numb I too leap toward the gate, and pull. The haoles and other people on the outside, for some strange reason, run up to the fence and start pulling. I pull because I am burning inside because I didn't tear down the HIC walls to see Joplin before she died. No! I am pulling because when I leaned back against the wall in class I was listening to a message that Lance was pounding out from the other side. I am pulling because of the way walls are so strategically placed, so remarkably calculated. I pull and feel the fence come crashing down. I see the husky guy whack Lenny with the flashlight. I jump him. Lenny grabs the flashlight, runs into the inside crowd, throws the flashlight, and when I see and hear the red spotlight shatter I cease to watch.

The Shadow Warrior

If he thought about it (perhaps he did; he never let on), he might have seen a pattern in the events of the last forty years, events that could be encapsulated within the opening and closing of a camera shutter, forming an imprint in his mind, which, of course, took it all in . . .

Isamaru Saga, semi-retired taxi driver, former photographer (his eyes got old), is setting up to take a family picture. He has balanced his tripod, mounted his 35 mm Nikon, and is focusing the lens, which is clearer than headlights, especially the painted headlights of the 1934 Studebaker that he last used as a taxi late in 1941, so late it was practically

[THE NIGHT OF NOH SHADOWS] 1942. Isamaru, wearing undershirt and shorts, could wait no longer for the next roundup. At 9:30 p.m., in the *dark* dark, he slipped on his trousers and (judging by the coconut buttons he felt) an aloha shirt. He then wiped his wire-rimmed glasses, put them on, and found his way to the front door. He grasped the door knob and turned it slowly.

"Whe' you going?" his wife, Tatsuyo, very pregnant, asked from behind him.

"I do' know . . . Ah-side."

"Ah-side?" Scolding: "*No* be stupid, now! Dey gon' arrest you. No can even see!"

"So? Good. Mo' bettah." He pushed the screen door and stepped out into the darkness.

"Mo' bettah? Kichigai man you . . ."

"Shaddup ah-ready." He slammed the screen door.

The blackout was in effect. Luckily, Isamaru knew the path to the Studebaker. He quietly opened the driver's door and got in. Started the car. The engine purred. Slowly he drove out the dirt lane to Hotel Street. He turned left, grimacing as the car scraped a rubbish can, then, squinting hard to see what lay ahead, he turned right, into Punchbowl. An invisible dog barked. Airplanes hummed muted roars that faded endlessly. Isamaru headed nervously toward Waikiki. Without the moon (lost behind a curtain of clouds) it was almost totally black. He glanced toward the invisible Koolaus and saw pinpricks of light. *Violators,* he thought. *They ought to be arrested.*

The headlights of the Studebaker were painted black around the edges and blue in the middle, as the military had ordered. Isamaru's "TAXI" sign lay somewhere on the large rear seat. He could not use it anymore, not since those *kichigai* warriors had swarmed to Pearl Harbor and punctuated his worst fears. When he turned right down Kalakaua Avenue, he knew that there was *no turning back.* He would drive through Waikiki and surely be rounded up. Like Reverend Tsuhako . . . Jimmy Yoshihara . . . Oshiro-san, his closest friend. "Why not me?" he had cried when Tatsuyo told him the searing news. *Why not me?* The words pounded like gongs against his temple.

He drove a steady twenty miles per hour down Kalakaua (which he knew like the backs of his unsteady hands), past McCully, past Fort DeRussy, where there seemed to be activity in the semi-dark (the cloud curtain no longer opaque but translucent). He thought to turn left at the fork, into the prong that was Kuhio Street, but chose to confront the situation head on and stayed on the main road.

The words on the Waikiki Theater marquee were imperceptible, but associations sufficed. The thought of John Wayne lassoing him by the neck gave him a jolt. Straightened his spine.

He braked. In the center of the road. He felt the pounding against his temples. He had no sword to defend himself. No cause. He squeezed the steering wheel tightly. Like a camera lens his glass-aided eyes panned for landmarks. He could see the vague outline of the Royal Hawaiian Hotel and further down, the Moana. No sailors, though. No loose wahines. *Why not me,* he said to

himself, feeling a rift, a tsunami forming within. "Why not me!"
he yelled. Then he trembled. A whisper: "Why not me?"

Nobody noticed. Even after he stepped on the gas and sped
two more times around. Finally, after heading *mauka* on Kapahulu
Avenue, he headed home.

After Isamaru parked the car he got out and began walking,
feeling his way to Beretania Street. (The location of his home
was destined to become part of the State Capitol lawn. Men in
large machines would come and knock down the entire camp, the
Armory, the service station, and then return later to take the dirt.)
He crossed the street and stopped at the wrought-iron cage that
surrounded Governor Poindexter's mansion. He could smell the
mock orange. Squeezing the iron bars with his hands, he peered in.
Nothing. He silently cursed his fate, cursed the darkness. (The
moon seemed to hear; it emerged, crescent, shining.)

"Cur-runch." The sound came from the dimly seen mock
orange bush. Isamaru stiffened like a cat, muscles taut, not
breathing.

Now, he thought, already feeling the rope around his neck.
And like a cat, a *cat* jumped through the iron bars, its eyes like
two sparkling swords.

"Mearrow," it said. Isamaru recaptured his breath.

"Heah, kiri-kiri," he whispered. The cat approached and
brushed against his pants leg. He knelt down, stroked its wiry
frame. It purred like the Studebaker right after a tune-up.

"Mea-arru." *No moon now.* Isamaru suddenly picked up the cat
(meeawrow?) and stole with this *koan* across the street and into
the warmer cold of the *unseen known.*

The lens cap wasn't removed until

[THE DAY OF NONE EITHER] 1952 when he panned his
Kodak Speed Graphic, then focused sharply on the unexpected,
new-born girl child. He peered through the lens, through the
large picture window, carefully selecting angles to avoid glare.
The hospital lights — diffuse — together with the high speed film
he used in his camera eliminated the need for flash. He took shot
after shot. The unexpectant mother and he, both in their forties
now, had not expected something this delightful so late in the ball

42

game. (Snap. Pan, focus; snap.) Their two daughters were seven and ten. (Pan, focus; snap. Snap.) He was as pinkly tickled as the Royal Hawaiian. (Snap.)

Through with the shooting, Isamaru went to the public telephone in the Queen's hospital corridor. The hospital smell reminded him of developing solution. He called Reverend Tsuhako, now safely ensconced in his Buddhist church in Makiki.

"Eh. Guess what?" Pause. "No, . . . girl." Isamaru laughed heartily. "No can make boy." More laughter. Pause. He said something in Japanese. Guffaws followed.

They named her Joy but would always call her by her middle name, Kyoko. Isamaru took an evening walk that day. Walks had become his refuge since the war days, a way of balancing darkness and light, a way to find the proper chiaroscuro, since everything had to be filtered by Hiroshima gray. As always he remembered to bring something along for cats to eat, should any cross his path. (The *mock orange* cat, by the way, fattened yet firm, had long ago left to embrace the *unknown seen.*)

Later, in his dark room he dipped the negatives one by one into solution. Darkness had become more familiar by now. (Perhaps it helped that his ten-year-old, a patient and eager assistant, was with him.) His job as photographer for a local Japanese newspaper provided enough for his family of four. Oops, five. He turned on the dim green light and gazed into the enlarger, turning the knob, expecting Joy. Instead he got (and it jolted him back) a man wearing a navy commander's cap and a confident smile.

JohnWayne? He roared when he realized what had happened.

"Whasamatta, daddy?" the ten-year-old asked.

"Look, look."

She looked into the enlarger. "Dass JohnWayne."

He laughed. The Duke himself was in town, making a movie called *Big Jim McClain.* He was no paniolo cowboy riding the range but rather a government agent investigating communist influence in Hawaii's longshoreman's union. Isamaru was assigned to get on-the-set photos. He was developing the wrong negatives. He straightened that out fast.

"I like do 'om, daddy."

"Be cah-ful."

"*I* know how," she said. He laughed again.

She did know. But she couldn't take too much of the alcohol-acid smell and finally left him alone in the red-tinged semi-dark to place the last sheet into the *unknown unseen.* He pulled the wet sheet out, in

[RAGGED SAMURAI, RIFT-RAFT, OR HELL IN THE PACIFIC] 1962, and hung it to dry.

"Daddy, we goin' show?" The spoiled ten-year-old asked.

"Shaddap. Wait." She smiled. *Wait* meant yes. She held her nose. She didn't like the *hospital* smell.

In the family Chevrolet station wagon (Studebaker long gone), Isamaru, with his little daughter (the older ones thought they had better things to do), sped down Nuuanu Avenue toward the Nippon Theater. He loved to see movies, especially samurai, or "chambara" films. Kyoko preferred "obake" movies, so she could grab her daddy's hand, scream, hide her face, and eat popcorn. Isamaru, being moved not by car wheels now but by film reels, basked in the increasingly comfortable darkness. *Sanjuro,* a Kurosawa film, was showing. Toshiro Mifune, his favorite actor, starred in it as a ragged samurai. He provided a nice antithesis to John Wayne, who had already made three films in Hawaii (Isamaru had photos to prove it) and was planning a fourth. Movie goers often referred to Mifune as Japan's John Wayne, though Isamaru's critic friend at *Hawaii Hochi* said

"Mifune is mo' like Brando."

Isamaru scratched his head. *"Nani?* What is Brando?"

To Isamaru, west was west and east was . . . supposed to be east. He was not too sure anymore. Something in the Kurosawa movies (which usually starred Mifune as the samurai with top knot shaven off, the samurai as thief, as riffraff addressed the rift, the drift he felt within. Was he doomed to float in the black Pacific on that raft, hiding a tsunami relentlessly westward? *As long as that raft held together* . . . Movies. Photography with *seams.*

Driving his daughter home in

[SUPER-DENSE] 1972, Isamaru said nothing. He had picked
Kyoko up at the police station cell block on Young Street. He had
put up the twenty-five dollars bail. She was now ranting about
the president . . . the War . . . the pigs . . . and on and on. She
wore her black hair long. She wore a white T-shirt with something
in Hawaiian printed on it, no bra, faded jeans, a black arm band
on her right sleeve. *No brah, you can't arrest me, you fucking jerk,
you*! She quoted herself.

Isamaru said nothing. He was a man of few words. He just
drove and drove until Kyoko realized that they weren't going
anywhere in particular but rather in circles. Or city squares. She
shut up. She looked at her father, whom she referred to (when
talking to friends) as being *super-dense,* whatever that meant.
Now he seemed *deep* (whatever *that* meant). She wanted to cry.
They drove through town, through Waikiki (where the Royal
Hawaiian was fast becoming a pinkie among poi-dipped fingers
and palms).

A taxi sign lay on the back seat of the 1971 Oldsmobile.
Isamaru's eyes were not what they used to be. He did not get
stronger glasses. He changed jobs.

Later, at home, Kyoko lay sleeping on the sofa. Isamaru bent
over her and checked her neck and arms for rope marks. He was
relieved to find none. At about midnight, unable to sleep, he took
a long walk to the State Capitol. He passed the Governor's
mansion (where friendlier forces seemed to dwell; until that day
at least) and walked toward the center mural where, he imagined,
Kyoko had been rounded up.

The mural was contained in a large circle; circles within
overlapped other circles. At center, Isamaru knelt in the semi-dark
to see better. The large circle and the circles within were made
up of tiny square tiles. Pieces.

JohnWayne wore a green beret now (Did his eyes get bad?).
In the sixties, with the help of his favorite director, John Ford,
he seemed to have realized that he was becoming larger than
life. Note the titles of his movies: *How The West Was won,
The Longest Day, The Greatest Story Ever Told, Cast A Giant
Shadow.* And he had licked cancer to boot.

Akira Kurosawa, on the other hand, was continuing (with
and without Mifune) to de-noble-ize the samurai. (The western

influence was prevalent. No wonder *Yojimbo* became the spaghetti western *A Fistful of Dollars,* and *Seven Samurai* became *The Magnificent Seven.*) Had he finally de-noble-ized his own stature as eminent Japanese director when in 1971 he attempted and failed to commit *seppuku?* A year earlier Yukio Mishima had exchanged the pen for the sword and had succeeded in his task for failing in his task.

But east is east, west is west.

And caught . . . in the middle . . . was Isamaru Saga.

(To explain his apoplexy, I was summoned to the hospital (in 1979 — shortly after the Duke finally succumbed to the Big C) to see if Isamaru was going to live or die. Luckily, it turned out to be a minor stroke. From the Kuakini hospital bed, room 304, Isamaru practically *ordered* me to go to the bakery to get him some pastry. Doughnuts and ladyfingers. I knew he was all right because I went.)

[KAGEMUSHA: THE SHADOW WARRIOR] 1982. He had parked his 1979 Ford in the second floor lot of the apartment building. Chewing on a piece of grass, he rode the elevator to the 22nd floor. He now drove taxi part time, the Honolulu *In-ta-na-sho-nar-ru* Airport his point of departure. He and Tatsuyo collected social security.

Isamaru slipped his key into the bolt lock, then opened the door.

"Surprise!" his daughter said.

"Eh? . . . How come?" Joy was there with her own little family: her husband, Rick, and their four-year-old son, Troy.

"We just thought we'd come visit," she said. Her haole husband smiled a cautious smile.

"Hi Ji-san," the little boy said, running up to his grandfather, who picked him up. Face to face with Troy, Isamaru grinned his silver and gold grin at this symbiosis, this . . . He put the boy down. Troy ran to the dining table and grabbed a package. "Look what I get fo' you."

"Fo' me?" It was a miniature metal car with a "TAXI" sign on top.

46

"We saw it at Sears," Joy said. "Troy kept saying 'Ji-san, Ji-san,' so we had to get it."

"Tangkyu." Isamaru bowed to his grandson. Troy, smiling proud, enjoyed giving. "You folks gon' stay fo' eat?"

"I guess so. You know mom." Tatsuyo was busy in the kitchenette of their one bedroom apartment. The government paid part of the rent. A John Wayne-like president was trying to lasso that away. "We were telling ma about this kid . . ." She pointed her thumb at Troy, who now sat on his father's lap. "Ever since we moved near the university, we have to take him up by the East-West Center 'cause he likes to look at the *koi* in the pool . . ."

"And the Indians," Rick said, laughing.

"In-dyens?" Isamaru looked puzzled.

"Oh yeah," Joy said. "Inside the Center. Not the bow and arrow kind, *da adda kine.*" Everyone laughed. "He seems entranced by the way they dress, not just Indians . . ."

"What about sistahs? Dey wen' write to you?" Tatsuyo asked from behind pots and steam.

"Not lately, dem buggahs." Talk centered on Joy's two older sisters, both also married and raising children. One lived on the island of Maui, while the other lived on the larger island known as the American continent, in some place called Kalamazoo. Then Tatsuyo announced:

"We need ketchup."

"Ketchup?"

"For Troy," Joy said. "He *has* to have it on his rice."

"On rice? Ketchup?" Isamaru scratched his head.

"I'll go buy some," Rick said as he and Troy got up. The first time Joy had brought her husband over to meet her parents, she said *This is Rick.* Her father grunted and left for a long walk.

"No. Dass okay," Isamaru said. "I take 'om."

"Yeah," Joy added. "Let dad take him. He has to take his walk." Rick looked puzzled. Joy and Tatsuyo laughed. "Yep . . . and his package."

"Walk? Package?"

Mother and daughter laughed harder.

"Nevah mind, you," Isamaru said as he grabbed a wrinkled package from the kitchen counter. Joy and Tatsuyo began to

47

explain as Isamaru and Troy slipped out the door.

"Don't buy him candy now!"

Isamaru was in the Pali Safeway store, walking down an aisle, carrying his package, some candy bars, and a bottle of ketchup in his hands. He was again chewing on a piece of grass. Troy, lingering behind, had picked up a sparkling silver pen, shiny as the gleam in his eyes. He ran to give it to his *Ojii-san*, his grandfather.

"No. Put back. Put back." Troy walked back slowly, while Isamaru went to the cashier. Troy stopped and put the pen in his pants pocket. He would give it to Ji-san later.

As they stepped outside a man grabbed Troy.

"Hey. Wha'samatta?"

"He stole a pen," the plainclothes guard said, and pulled it out of Troy's pocket. "See? and could I see what's in that package?"

"You crazy o' what? He only one . . ." Troy began to cry.

"Please come with me." Isamaru felt the guard's hand choking his arm. He decided to comply.

The manager came up and asked the guard what was going on.

"The kid stole this pen." He gave it to the manager. "And the old man has a package that . . ."

"Let me see." The manager reached out for the package. Isamaru gave it to him. The manager opened it. "Let's see . . ." He saw a can opener, a saucer, and a can of cat food. "Oh, Christ. Some thief. We don't even sell this brand." He looked at the guard, shaking his head. "He's only a kid. He doesn't know what stealing is. My own son has picked up things."

"Sorry, I'm just trying to . . ." The guard's face was flushed.

"We're sorry," the manager said, cutting the guard off. Isamaru, who had been rubbing his grandson's head, was gazing out into the parking lot at a car that reminded him of the Studebaker. "You folks can go on. It's just a mistake."

Isamaru pushed up his glasses and looked at the manager. "Mistake! Eretime, mistake! No care how much harm!" He grabbed his package, his red-eyed grandson, and stalked away toward the nearby drugstore. *Seen. Known.*

They knew him there, where he developed negatives, bought cat food. Isamaru walked toward the stationery section and picked up two silver pens.

"One fo' me," he told Troy. "An' one fo' you." The cashier told him he had a handsome grandson. Why *not* me.

Two happy warriors walked out of the store. Alongside a bush near the apartment, Isamaru looked around then opened his package. He opened the cat food can, poured the contents onto the plate, and set it down. Two cats came out from the bushes.

"Here kitty-kitty," the little warrior gurgled. His smile was like water. Isamaru laughed when Troy tapped the cat's head with his pen.

Isamaru is not content with the Nikon and digs out his trusty Speed Graphic. He removes its flash and aluminum shield. Then he sets up a lamp behind him. Everyone is getting restless. *Hurry up, dad. Just take the picture.*

Finally he does take the picture. But not before he pushes his son-in-law, me, further into it.

But Isamaru has bigger things on his mind. While Joy and I browse through the family photo albums and "mama" cleans up in the kitchenette, "dad" poses Troy and the pen, trying to capture shadows on the wall. The miniature taxi looms large. So does the pen when Troy holds it right. The scene is contrived, but so is the opening scene of *Kagemusha,* Kurosawa's latest movie.

But Isamaru gets no sword and finally sees, accepts, that what is cast on the wall is Troy's own. It is in this final letting go that Isamaru Saga ends *his* saga. As he presses for the shot, whispering "Kuroshii," *I am done,* and as whatever-it-is is cast onto the wall, *shimmering,* I find myself, unseen, undone, caught in the target of a Zen archer.

The Ties That Bind

Miles Away

The heat was getting to him.

And it did not help that the cool, blue West Loch of Pearl Harbor loomed so tantalizingly in the killer August heat. And that he was hungry and that the warm water from the outdoor tap didn't quite quench his thirst. And it did not help Jeff to think about having spent the whole summer working as cheap labor for his dad, a masonry contractor, to earn (if he'd even get paid!) his college tuition. And neither did it help Jeff to think of the mad drunkenness he'd seen in his father's eyes at each day's end, which for his father was sundown, not four-thirty or five o'clock, like for most normal human beings.

And it did not make it any cooler for Jeff to think about how his father yelled at him so much. Or to think about it being Friday, the end of the week for most people. For his dad there was no end, no rest, only the cycle of work, followed by work, then more work.

The heat was getting to him.

The day had started bad enough. Getting up, in that sorry excuse for a house on Mokauea Street in Kalihi, rushing through the same eggs and toast meal his mother fixed up every morning, and, within minutes, heading out in that crusty old Ford pickup that buckled along toward whatever lame highway that would lead to another lame suburb where Jeff and his dad would build another wall, patio, or some other cement modification to a house to extend it beyond its original possibilities.

Like just about every day for the past couple of months, Jeff attempted to circumvent the dreary routine by inventing more

pleasurable ones of his own. His latest thing was to count Volkswagens that he saw along the way—whether they passed from
the other direction, moved along in traffic with his dad's pickup,
or lay idle on some streetside. He took care not to count the same
one more than once, though this was difficult sometimes with the
cars that went in the same direction.

Usually he counted up to forty or fifty by the time they arrived
at their destination. Today, when they had reached Pacific
Palisades, a suburb way up in the hills above Pearl City, he had
barely reached thirty. It was going to be that kind of day.

Jeff's father gave him the usual assignments—continue digging
the twenty by twenty-five foot area where the patio is going to be
six inches deep, then dig a twelve-to-sixteen-inch wide footing
for the retaining wall, allowing for steps at the marked places,
then start stacking the hollow tile, twenty for every four feet—
then he left mumbling something about picking up more something—maybe it was sand. Jeff could never understand his father's
mumblings, and was tired of being scolded for not understanding,
for being "so damn dumb fo' one kid who like go college" that he
now chose not to ask.

Sometimes he chose to guess rather than ask, even when he
knew he'd guess wrong. Like the time his father mumbled something to Jeff about getting him a "groovah" and Jeff didn't know
what it was or if he had even heard right and so he resolved it
by grabbing something unfamiliar from the tool box and his
father said "No. I said da 'groovah'!" and Jeff said *Oh* and went
and got another wrong tool and received more scolding, his father
saying, "What dey teach you in school? You dunno what one
'groovah' is?" His father went and showed him.

But it was better than seeing the look on his father's face
when he said "What?"

Jeff dug for an hour or two before his father returned with
red eyes, muttering something incoherent about forgetting something, and left again. Then Jeff continued his digging, wiping his
face with his T-shirt periodically because he was already perspiring
a lot in the mid-morning heat.

He liked it when his father was gone. Better than him being
around scolding him all the time. At that moment though, the
thought that his father may have been drinking didn't even enter

54

Jeff's mind. Then, about an hour later, when his father returned, this time with sand—something to show, at least—Jeff noticed very clearly the irrationality, the dim madness that had begun to overcome his dad.

"Staht unloading da sand," his father said, fairly coherently. "I gotta go back an' get some rock."

Jeff abandoned the trench he had been digging and dragged the shovel on over to the pickup to unload the truckload of sand onto the driveway while his father checked the fruits of his son's previous labor with his steel tape measure. Then his father went and got his thermos from the cab of the truck and poured himself a cup of coffee—all he drank *on* the job—and watched his son scoop shovelful after shovelful of sand with mild disapproval. Then he poured the remaining half a cup on the clean garage floor, grabbed another shovel, and started scooping sand from the rear of the truck alongside his son. "You nevah goin' finish li' dat," he said as he scooped heaping shovelfuls of sand at a furious pace, spilling a lot. Jeff tried to keep up and tried also to avoid the occasional *clang* when both of their shovels vied for the same space. Then he grabbed a broom to sweep the remaining thin layer of sand from the truckbed.

Afterwards, Jeff's father repeated his orders, showed him where he had dug too little, and left to get a load of rock.

When he was sure his father was gone, Jeff gave himself a short break. He drank water from the tap, sat on a nearby wall wiping the sweat off his face, and gazed down at Pearl Harbor's West Loch.

He began feeling sorry for himself, cursing his fate. He was aware that some of his friends—college tuition all saved up by conscientious parents—were out in something that was as cool and wet and blue as the ocean he could see beyond, riding waves that crested, rolled, re-formed. As for the others, friends who had to work like he did, at least they didn't have to slave like he did, working long hours, weekends too.

"The summer I missed all the waves," he mumbled to himself in the standard English he reserved for specious occasions. It sounded like the title of a freshman English paper.

Freshman at the University. That thought loomed as enticing, as teasingly vague, as the horizon . . . that single line, that crossing . . . over into what? He tried to picture the pristine classes, with rows and rows of beautiful coeds. But it was all a blur, just a tease, and perhaps would be till he got there.

And would he get there? With a father like his, who knew?

And where was his father?

Jeff got hot just thinking that this time his jackass of a father had gone too far. It was getting on into the afternoon and he still hadn't returned. It must have been past lunchtime, his stomach making that claim. Finally, Jeff swiped a few mangoes from a nearby tree. He was really hungry but he didn't want to scrounge from the Browns, the people — or customers, as his father referred to all those he worked for — they were building the patio and wall for. Jeff was sure that the Browns were already wondering about his father's disappearing act, as other customers had done previously.

Even though Jeff had already done everything his father had assigned him to do — stack the tile, dig the footing and the patio area — he still tried to look busy. Jeff didn't want his father to arrive, catch him goofing off and yell at him, telling him again what a hopeless, no-good, idiot of a son he was. So he remeasured every place he'd dug, recounted every stack of tile . . . and then he did it all again. This seemed to go on for hours. In between, Jeff threw pebbles into the trench he had dug, or at mangoes, inventing games, anything to distract himself.

Finally, Jeff concluded that even *his* father had to be able to understand that there was absolutely nothing else for him to do, so he sat down. And waited.

And waited. Wiping the sweat off his brow every now and then. Finally, Jeff decided to walk on over to his weird auntie's house.

Actually the ex-wife of his dead uncle, his Auntie Julie was the closest living relative residing within the reasonable distance of a hike in the Palisades area. She lived about a half mile away.

Jeff had to envy the suburbs. He saw children playing in their large, green yards, or shooting basketballs into hoops built over garages. He could hear the rocking sounds of a garage band practicing somewhere. He saw toddlers splashing in plastic wading pools, cooling off from the heat, and teenagers who did not have to work like he did, hosing their cars down.

When Jeff arrived at his auntie's house, he found her sitting
at the kitchen table, along with her three adult sons. Two of them,
he knew, had served prison terms. For what crimes, he had no
idea. Jeff used to have a morbid fear of his cousins, the notorious
Ahakuelo brothers, but had finally gotten used to the idea that they
weren't inclined to rob, mug, or mutilate their young cousin—as
long as he played it straight with them. In fact, once he'd find
himself conversing with one of them, he found it to be reassuring.
He'd even feel glad that he was related to them. Like it was . . .
protection. Jeff let himself believe that there was a code: cousins
don't hurt cousins . . . unless.

And Jeff wasn't about to do no "unless."

"Hey, cousin," Larry, the largest and oldest one, said. He wore
no shirt, and Jeff could see the scar across his midsection. Some
appendix operation, Jeff thought. Jeff greeted his cousin with a
quick glance. Even when Larry smiled, his eyes looked dangerous.
Distant, calculating . . . prisoner's eyes. Jeff also noticed—not for
the first time—his cousin's smashed nose and wild, curly hair.

"Hey, Jeffrey. Watchu doin' up here?" This was Junior, the
good-looking one. *Could have been an actor,* relatives used to
grumble, *if he wasn't so damn hopeless like the rest of his—*

"Gee," auntie cut in, "at least you come visit us."

Jeff thought that his cement-pocked T-shirt—sleeves cut off—
and his dirt-stained jeans were a clue that he hadn't just come
visiting. He hoped that they'd offer him food, but a ride home
would certainly do.

"You like some coffee?" auntie said. Jeff shook his head.

"Nah, ma. Da kid like one beer." This was Miles, the other
ex-con, speaking. He wore mirror sunglasses.

"No t'anks," Jeff managed to say. He felt like a kid. "Uh . . .
(he now had their attention—*how to say it*) my faddah lef' me fo'
do some work . . . an' he nevah come back."

Miles and Junior looked at each other and grinned. Junior
said, "Oh, uncle stay hitting da booze again." He said this with his
hand balled into a fist, thumb sticking out, gesturing toward his
mouth. They knew.

"Bad enough working fo' him when he straight," Miles said,
laughing. "I hear he one slave drivah."

Yeah. But at least he not dead, Jeff wanted to say. What he did say was: "Yeah, I was figuring he wasn't coming back so I bettah get home."

Then in from the hallway walked a tall, bosomy blonde woman who Jeff didn't recognize. She smiled when she saw Jeff. Then she announced, "Well, I'm leaving. . . ."

"Wait, Melissa," Jeff's auntie said. "I t'ink da kid need one ride. Dis my nephew, Jeffrey." Again Melissa smiled. "You goin' down da highway, eh?"

Kid. The word stung.

"Oh, yeah," Jeff said. "Sure."

"You know Melissa?" Jeff shook his head. "She Junior's girl-friend. She work at Pearlridge. Dis my nephew, Jeffrey," she said again.

"Hi, Jeffrey."

"Hi."

"Well," Junior said, "you can take my cousin down to da highway, den he can catch one bus." Junior looked at Jeff. "You get money fo' bus?" Jeff nodded, lying.

"Come on, let's go," Melissa said.

As Jeff headed out he wondered why he had lied. Was it because he didn't like riding buses and would rather hitch a ride home on the highway? Or was it because he already felt so much like a kid, more so with Melissa, who was perhaps just a year or two older than he was, and yet looked so ripe, alluring, mature.

And grownups carry cash, for Christ's sake! At least enough for the bus!

Later, at age twenty, Jeff, then a promising college student, would remember Melissa in the glazed blue eyes of another blonde, and think—circumstances being more convenient—that he could have easily gotten into her panties. *Just get'em stoned and . . .* But a few years later, when school had gotten too crazy and too disillusioning and he'd again become part of the work force, this time in an air-conditioned office full of young females of all skin tones, body shapes, and temperaments, when he'd understood how the mass media set the standards as far as beauty was concerned and had made reconciliations of his own, he'd think back and understand that she would have dismissed any advances quickly enough, for by then he knew about *the tease.*

Yet still, years later, when Jeff saw her for the first time in years at a funeral, when he'd learned from his mom that Junior had been killed while trying to block the path of a bullet with his head, Melissa looked so jaded, pregnant and splotchy as she was, that he wondered how he ever could have been so attracted to her, yet at the same time wanting again to be her shining knight, rescuing her and Junior, *Jr.* (whether boy or girl), pulling them out of that vicious circle, yet painfully knowing better. . . .

But it probably wasn't till he was thirty, when he had spurned the easy attention of the hot-to-trot, nineteen-year-old daughter of a customer whose house he, a self-employed carpenter, was making modifications to, spurning her because he had learned the hard habit of looking into the ramifications of each action he took, that he had also learned one important lesson: *just because sex is always on your teenage mind it doesn't mean it's on anyone else's.*

In any case, when Melissa opened the door to her light blue Volkswagen, leaning over from the driver's seat, smiling at Jeff, her blouse loose, exposing her breasts, she looked like her name might be "Unless."

Less intimidated by her presence now that her cousins and auntie weren't around, Jeffrey enjoyed the doubly scenic drive down and around the mountain that the community of Pacific Palisades sat on. He used to dream of maybe one day riding his skateboard down the bending, descending and rising road, breathlessly riding, making a blur of the austere, shrubbery-strewn mountainscape. . . . This blur now formed the backdrop to the light hairs on the light skin of the woman he sat next to . . . where, like the backdrop, there too were slopes . . and crevices. *Light years away.*

Melissa's skin wasn't the best. It was too light to have seen much Hawaiian sunshine, like she didn't know how nice it could be when you blended sand and sun and surf, but Jeff felt that that bit of imperfection made her more accessible. No . . . real. No. . . . He didn't know.

"So," she said. "You got stranded."

"Yeah. I t'ink my dad got too drunk." It was only then that Jeff thought of the word "accident," and wondered if he should be worried.

59

"My dad drinks a lot, too. . . . So does Junior. I wish he'd straighten up and not be like his brothers. . . ." Melissa took a quick look at Jeff after she had negotiated an uphill turn. "You have such nice shoulders. Do you surf?"

"Ah, not lately." Jeff looked at her. Her eyes were intent on the road. This enabled him to stare, absorb, remember. They were on a straightaway now, a steep downhill ride that she handled in third gear. He wanted to say *You have nice shoulders, too. You have a lot of nice things,* but he refrained.

Jeff also wanted to tell her that her chances would be better with someone like him, someone who'd know how to treat a girl right, someone who had a future. But in his dirty clothes, with his hair all cement-spattered, his wallet empty, he knew he was an unlikely candidate for knight-in-shining-armor status. Besides, who was rescuing whom? This is not me, Jeff wanted to say. I'm miles away from this.

Traffic was heavy when Melissa dropped Jeff off at the highway's edge. Everyone was through work. He wanted to kiss her goodbye. It seemed only right. But then he thought about her name being "Unless."

Jeff hitched a ride home. It wasn't hard. With traffic so slow he could easily make eye-contact with strangers and, surely enough, one would see the gloom in his eyes and pick him up.

Jeff didn't get a blonde this time, much less a woman. The *blalah,* the burly Hawaiian that picked him up seemed friendly enough though, and was headed toward Kalihi himself. After a while, Jeff realized that this guy had been drinking. It wasn't that he was incoherent or anything like that. He just was obvious. He opened a package and pulled out a can of Schlitz. He offered Jeff some brew. "No t'anks," Jeff muttered.

"So yo' faddah lef' you stranded?" the driver said in a surprisingly high-pitched voice. And as he talked he nodded to some rhythm only he heard. Then he let out a long belch.

"I dunno. Maybe somet'ing wen' happen. Car trouble o' somet'ing."

"'Ass why hard." The driver opened the can of Schlitz. Jeff noticed how his T-shirt failed to cover his protruding stomach. At least, Jeff thought, at least my dad only lets it get to his head.

"You leef?" the driver said.

What? Leaf?

"You pump iron, brah?"

Oh. "Yeah . . . I mean, no."

The driver looked at him curiously. "Me neidah." Strained conversation.

There was little else for the two to talk about during the long drive home. At one point the blalah tried to talk baseball and Jeff tried to sound enthused.

"Dodgers won, eh? Las' night."

"Oh yeah? All right." Jeff didn't really care about how the Dodgers were doing right then.

"Who you t'ink goin' win da pennant, dem o' da Astros?"

"Dodgers, I hope," Jeff said, getting the drift.

"All right! You all right, bruddah." The driver tapped Jeff's shoulder with his beer-enclosed hand, spilling about a fourth of a full can on Jeff's arm. Then he swallowed the rest of the contents, crushed the can in his hand, and threw it on the passenger-side floor, adding to the growing pile of cans. "No good littah, eh?"

Jeff nodded, wishing the truck had a radio.

Jeff's mother stood behind the screen door when he came trudging home past sundown. "Your faddah's in jail," she said with appropriate melodrama, "and he's gonna stay dere. I not bailing him out."

Jeff wondered what his father could have possibly done. And he felt relieved that he himself was not in trouble.

Later Jeff found out that his father had been arrested for drunk driving after he had knocked over, in succession, a street lamp, a mail box, a piece of somebody's garage, as well as the bird of paradise flowers in someone's prized garden. This happened on Young Street, miles away from where he was supposed to be. Witnesses said he had been tooting his horn, perhaps even laughing, as he drove through people's yards and on sidewalks. "Let him sleep it off in jail," his mom said. She had had enough of his drinking sprees.

That night Jeff went out, really out. The more he worked for his dad, the weirder it got working with him, the more "out there" he had to get. Hanging out with friends, listening to loud music,

passing joints deep into the night; refusing beer, checking out the
Doors, checking out the Stones, Neil Young and Crazy Horse, anybody, as long as it was strong, loud, numbing. That night especially, especially after the brief conversation he had had with his
mother before a friend had picked him up. She had been crying.

"I dunno how he goin' pay fo' your tuition. He stay spending
all his money on liquor."

"Dass all right, ma."

"He neglecting da bills." Jeff hated the man even more.

"Dass all right, ma."

At five the next morning Jeff heard the voice of his father,
calling him. "Come on. Get up. We get work fo' do."

Oh, no. Please, God. No. It can't be.

Jeff had stayed up late with friends, had smoked too many
joints, and had dropped off to sleep only a few hours earlier. He
wanted to weep. He could shake off the fit of sleep, the unfinished
dream, the uncomfortable ache in his bones, but not the intense
hate he felt toward his father.

There was no time for breakfast, his father told him. Jeff
quickly washed up and got dressed and went out to help his father
load. They threw a couple of wheelbarrows, shovels, and some
smaller tools onto the truckbed and headed out — while the sun sat
frozen in the east — toward the freeway, with Jeff again cursing
his fate and redoubling his desire to get away from the madman
as soon as, in any way, he could.

Jeff did not want to ask his father how he managed to get
out of jail; he did not want to talk. He just did what he had to do
— count Volkswagens. Except that this time, the world being
harsher, he looked through the dew-laced windshield of every
Volkswagen for the beautiful face of Melissa, or any exotic cutey.
Anything to obliterate reality.

When they arrived on the job-site, Jeff's father scanned the
layout his son had designed and muttered the only word that Jeff
was ever to hear from him in praise: "Good. . . . Now staht
digging one step ovah here. An' . . ." indicating with a shovel,
". . . one mo' ovah here. We gotta make two mo' steps." Then,
like a politician breaking new ground, his father scooped up the
first shovelful, then stabbed the blade of the shovel into the

ground where he wanted his son to dig and went to get himself a cup of coffee.

By then it was six-fifteen. The cement truck was scheduled to arrive at seven. Mr. Brown, the owner of the house, an elderly man with a gardener's tan, came running out.

"Oh, for Christ's sake," he said. "Are you planning to go ahead? You're not even ready! I get a call from HC&D. They say a truck is coming. And you're not even ready. . . . For Christ's sake."

Jeff's father muttered something incomprehensible, then farted, a lengthy, sonorous wooze of a fart. Then he looked at Jeff, who had stopped for a moment. "Come on. No waste time."

"Look," the owner said, "you can't go ahead with this. If you ruin my property, I swear, I'll sue you."

Jeff's father did not respond. He grabbed some pegs, nails, and a hammer and began to set the lumber frame for the patio.

"This is the worst —" the owner started to say, then he stormed into his house.

Jeff's father seemed to take it all in, swallowing it humbly. He continued setting the frame while Jeff dug the two six-inch steps where his father had indicated. Then his father called to him to help him lay out the screen on the ground where the patio was going to be. The wire screen came in a large, fifteen-foot-wide roll. Because it tended to roll up, having been in that set so long, it was necessary for Jeff and his dad to twist it in the other direction.

By now Jeff felt comfortable because of the familiarity of the routine. He even allowed himself to think that his father knew exactly what he was doing. He also allowed himself to think about the horrors that his old man must have lived through. He knew about the Sunday morning in Kalihi when his then young father had to stop delivering ice in order to toss wounded bodies into passing cars, the morning of the attack of Pearl Harbor. He had also heard about his father witnessing Japanese friends in post-World War Two Germany, where he had been stationed, being beaten by white American GIs because these GIs couldn't tell these Asian-Americans apart from the *Japs* who blasted Pearl Harbor although *he,* standing on the side, feeling so uncomfortably brown, could tell a white American from a white German from a white

Frenchman. . . . And Jeff also knew about the one single thing that almost killed his father: the sudden death of the infant sister Jeff never knew, the sister who died before Jeff had been conceived, much less considered.

But what Jeff didn't know, could never know, perhaps, was what was it that made his father want to douse the flames of his existence with alcohol and, in effect, feed the churning fire?

And Jeff thought about all the joints he had sucked deep into his soul the night before.

Then it started to rain. Jeff was no longer tired, fatigue being an unnecessary luxury at the moment. He could hear the cement truck coming up the mountain road. Straining.

Jeff's mind moved with the frantic haste of their actions as he and his father raced to cover the area they had prepared for the patio with tarp.

Then the other men—Fidel, Masa, and Joe—arrived. Fidel often helped Jeff's dad on weekends, especially when he needed someone strong to push another wheelbarrow. He was built like a tractor. Masa was the expert finisher. Retired already, he worked with Jeff's dad only when he needed to do a floor or patio. Masa and his dad could make a floor so smooth you didn't want to even breathe on it, fearing a breath could ruin the perfection. But, once it was dry, you'd want it to be your dance floor.

Jeff didn't know Joe. He too was well-muscled, and had greasy, slicked-back hair that looked like he only used his fingers to comb it. Jeff wondered how his father had arranged all this, having spent the night sauced in a jail cell.

Again Jeff could hear the straining of the cement truck, this time louder. Mr. Brown came out again, sheltering his head from the rain with one arm. "I can't let you do this!" he shouted to Jeff's dad. "I can't let you ruin my—"

His wife had come out also. She was fat and maternal-looking under her umbrella. The rain was now a refreshing drizzle. "Harry, let them do it. Come on. Let them alone." Her tone told Jeff that she also thought they were screwing up, but felt that there was no sense in making things worse.

Jeff had finished the steps and asked his father, "What now?"

"Get da tools ready. Da shovels . . . wash da wheelbarrows
. . . an' no pour da watah on da grass, now. Go by da drain." Jeff's

father looked up at the rain coming down and shook his head, as if thinking maybe this time even he could not pull it off.

Then the cement truck arrived. And behind it a beat-up car with three large men inside. The cement truck driver got out and turned on the mix switch. Jeff watched the gigantic barrel spinning to the appropriate mixture—not too soupy, his dad would always say—of sand, water, cement and gravel. The three men got out of the rusted-out Chevrolet. They were Jeff's cousins, Larry, Miles, and Junior. They were all shirtless, and they all wore rubber slippers.

"Hey uncle," Miles yelled. He still wore his mirror sunglasses. "You guys need help?"

"We saw da truck coming up," Junior said to Jeff, "so we wen' follow yom."

"Ey, cuz," Larry said to Jeff. Again those killer eyes. "Workin' hard?"

Jeff's father had gazed up through the rain, praying for divine assistance, the stuff of angels. Devils were sent instead, but they'd do. He told his nephews they could either help wheelbarrow or help shovel dirt on the places where puddles were forming. There was a job to do.

The pace was now accelerated. Through the drizzle, Jeff watched the seven men grab shovels, wheelbarrows, Masa and his dad putting on their rubber boots to wade in the concrete. Before Jeff knew it, everything was taken. He was left with nothing tangible to do. And he wanted badly to do something. He stood in the midst of the frenzy: Miles, Fidel, and Joe practically running with wheelbarrowloads of concrete, Larry and Junior shoveling like crazy.

Finally, Jeff asked his father, who stood frantically shoveling in the middle of the concrete, making mold out of mud, what he could do. "Help 'om pour," his father said as he continued shoveling.

Jeff did what he would call, years later, "make-work," superfluous work, the kind of work one does when there's too many workers—rearrange files, put new labels on them when there's nothing wrong with the old ones. The kind of work that did slow damage to the arteries, finally the hearts, if not the souls, of civil servants. Jeff helped guide the concrete pouring down the trough

65

extending to the wheelbarrows, scraping the excess that often dripped on to the ground with a stick.

Then when Joe — he had been clumsy anyway, spilling stuff all over thoughtlessly — abandoned his wheelbarrow to help Masa and Jeff's dad do the finishing, Jeff quickly grabbed hold of its two handles, now — unlike before — with a sense of assurance and control. He hardly spilled a drop. There were no more son and wheelbarrow episodes that made Jeff's father shake his head and others laugh, no more crying "I can't . . . too heavy. . . ." Now Jeff realized that his muscles had been growing, imperceptibly, steadily, all summer long. No wonder the 94-pound cement bags had seemed to have gotten lighter, no wonder he could now carry *two* thirty-eight pound hollow tiles in each hand while stacking, no wonder Melissa and the blalah had commented . . .

The cement truck driver poured fuller and fuller loads into Jeff's wheelbarrow. Jeff felt great as he practically ran with the load over the slippery, hazardous course to dump it at whatever spot his father indicated. When Jeff lifted to unload, he felt the symmetry and grace of a weightlifter doing bench presses on a *Universal.* And when he went back for another load, as the driver pulled the lever and the concrete that was pouring out threatened to topple the wheelbarrow, Jeff held on to the two handles, flexed, feeling for the moment that one arm needed to hold tighter, pull harder, to compensate for the shifting weight, balanced, like a surfer waiting for a wave.

By now, Jeff was the only one pushing a wheelbarrow. The others had probably quit from exhaustion. Or felt that they had done enough. Or were helping to shovel the concrete. "One mo' load," Jeff's father shouted finally, indicating that only one load would be needed to finish the patio. The driver nodded, then proceeded to fill Jeff's wheelbarrow to the brim. It seemed as though all eyes were on Jeff as he pushed the ridiculously heavy load on toward the indicated edge. Time slowed down. Everyone seemed to share the same heartbeat. The Ahakuelo brothers, Masa, Joe, Fidel, even his dad stopped to watch the kid. Jeff thought of balance. Nothing else. Everything else a haze of "it-doesn't-matter." Then his mind flashed on "Unless." He slipped, but pulled one side up quick and hard to regain his balance, feeling the terrible strain on his lower back.

66

Again, the heat got to him, this time the heat of the eyes upon him. He felt angry. *What?* he silently told all who gazed at him, judging him. *You wanna see?* His legs were churning, the backs of his thighs straining, as he pushed the wheelbarrow up the slippery plank. *Wanna see something bad, eh?* He negotiated the uneasy turn with a quick lateral shift, thinking only of the need for it to be balanced . . . balanced. Then he pulled upward, releasing the entire contents in one cathartic surge, twisting the handles as his father scraped the remains from the sides of the wheelbarrow.

"All right!" Larry and Miles said harmoniously.

"Give the kid a prize," Junior echoed.

"Piece a' cake," Jeff muttered as he dragged the empty wheelbarrow away. He went to get a long drink of water. Junior and Miles came to drink also. There was a spot of cement on Junior's forehead, just above the spot where, years later, a bullet would end his life. Jeff turned to look at Miles, but all he could see, in the mirror sunglasses, was an image of himself that was more distant than Larry's eyes.

Afterwards, while his dad and Masa, everyone else excused for the day, did the final smoothing out of the patio, Jeff washed down everything. The rain had remained a light drizzle throughout, and had finally stopped. Jeff washed out the wheelbarrows, the shovels, the pegs and lumber, the finishing tools — the darby, the edger, he knew the names now.

Jeff looked around to see if there was anything else to wash. Not finding anything, he held the hose down over his head and washed himself. He wanted to wash down his father's truck, wash down his cousins, the other men, the Browns, everything, the washing felt so good.

Mr. Brown came out. "I hate to admit it," he said, muttering, to Jeff's father, "but . . . gee . . . great job. I'm sorry about earlier. I should have banked on your reputation. . . ."

Jeff's dad barely nodded to acknowledge the apology and praise. For him it seemed to be everyday . . . the challenge, the testing, the imminent threat of failure . . . then, but barely, the triumph, however modest it may be. If anything, Jeff's dad seemed weary. These accomplishments had become routine, so he had to invent ways of making it harder, more of a challenge, he had to take it even closer to the edge, just to make it interesting.

Once everything was loaded on the truck, Jeff's father came up to him. Masa was already sitting in the cab, on the passenger side. "Made pretty good money on dis job," Jeff's father said. "I like doing patios, floors . . . easy." Jeff's mother was to tell her son later, much later, when she herself found out, that this job had paid for his tuition.

Jeff sat in the truckbed, his back against the cab's rear window, as they rode down and around the mountain — heading home. In the blur of the landscape he saw the entire summer whizzing by. He wondered what time it was. The sun was blazing overhead, a bit to the east. Perhaps ten thirty. Pearl Harbor, and the ocean beyond, looked inviting, decked out as they were in Jeff's favorite blues. He was hungry, his stomach told him. He knew they'd stop somewhere and get something to eat. They always did. Then Jeff would still have the whole day in front of him, a day of sand and surf. Without the cement. *All right. Maybe I should start counting shades of green . . . or brown,* Jeff said to himself as they jaunted by the dry mountainside. *Or Toyotas. There's plenty of those.* Then Jeff smiled, his face turned away from the two silent old men in front, as he saw a sky blue Volkswagen downshifting by and accelerating oceanward in the tropical heat.

Under the Table

May 1969

Maybe we weren't listening. Or just couldn't understand. It was often like that in school. So, when the teachers passed out exams, we'd look at the questions, give each other funny looks, then proceed to cheat.

On this occasion, we were almost through taking a test in our American Problems class at Farrington High. We were the class of '69, a precious two and a half weeks away from graduation. Mrs. Harada, our teacher, had trusted us enough to leave the classroom temporarily, leaving Marsha Olayan (Marsha the Brain, we called her; she always finished taking tests first) to act as monitor. What the teacher didn't know was that Marsha had a mean crush on Lenny Batista, the cheating scheme ringleader, and as soon as Marsha was in charge, pieces of paper that had been carefully passed from one student to another now flew around the room like paper planes.

Sometimes cheating was too easy. As a class we seemed to be arriving at the notion that it was more fun to come up with the answers on our own. And in the case of this test, when I started to do just that, I found myself both tickled and puzzled by one peculiar question. It read: "What world leader in 1959 made the statement, 'We will bury you,' thus feeding the fire of the Cold War?" Knowing the answer, for once, I started to write it down. Then, unsure of the spelling of the foreign name, I picked up the paper airplane that had landed in front of me seconds earlier. I opened it up and read the words that were etched in almost calligraphic style. It read: ANSWER TO #17 — NICKY DA CRUISE JOB. I coughed out a laugh and thought immediately:

69

Lenny. I looked across the table, where he sat, but he wasn't there. Puzzled, I shook my head—perhaps chiding myself in advance for what I was about to do—crossed out what I had started to write, and wrote "Nicky da Cruise Job." Then I felt something tugging at my pant cuffs. Normally I would have kicked. But I knew it had to be Lenny. I dropped my pen—on purpose—and went under the table to get it.

So there we were, amidst the flurry of legs. Bare female legs, covered male ones. We sat eight to a table, so there were twelve legs left to surround us. Just at the moment that Lenny motioned for me to look in the direction of Lynette Toma's crotch, I whispered "Nicky da Cruise Job" and he gulped down a laugh and suddenly we were in the sixth grade.

May 1963

I couldn't understand it when Miss Lake told us we had to go under the table because of Nicky da Cruise Job. She said if we didn't hide under the table that Nicky da Cruise Job was going to bomb us guys. So we'd be under the table, our lessons totally disrupted—to our excitement and delight—and I'd be wondering, Who is this guy, Nicky da Cruise Job?

Finally, one Friday after school, I asked Lenny, figuring he was almost as smart as Shane but at least he doesn't punch you when you ask questions. I had to ask Lenny because it was like I had been absent and I had missed something and I hated that feeling. But Lenny said he didn't know either. He said that Larry Kanahele had told him that Miss Lake actually pronounced it, "Nicky da Cruise Chef," not "Nicky da Cruise Job," and that Nicky da Cruise, Job or Chef, was actually a Mafia guy and that this Mafia guy Nicky da Cruise had a chef working for him like Larry's Uncle Keoki who worked as a chef at the Queen's Surf in Waikiki.

All I could figure out was that I had to ask Shane and risk getting punched. Since it was Friday, I knew I'd see Shane the next day when he and Gerry and Lenny and me were going to see an Elvis Presley matinee at a theater downtown.

Perseverance was the ticket to a movie those days. That is, if you nagged your mom until she realized that not having you around was worth the buck and a half—two bucks, if she felt rich

70

—that would get you there.

We were meeting at the bus stop near the corner of King and Kalihi streets, in front of the Kamehameha Homes Public Housing Project (a low-income development whose name everyone shortened to Kam Housing), across Farrington High School. Me and Gerry were always the first ones there.

"Maybe like 'De la Cruz.' You know, like Gerry's last name," Gerry was saying, referring to another Gerry. He was wearing a new pair of Levi's that had about twenty pockets. And from the pocket that ran alongside from below his right hip to just short of his knee, Gerry pulled out a long, black comb and began to comb his thick-with-pomade black hair.

"No, but . . . da teachah said 'Cruise Job' . . . I t'ink. Shit, I dunno."

We were going to see *It Happened At The World's Fair* at the King Theater. While a war movie or cowboy movie sounded more exciting, we went along with Shane's fervent wish to see the latest Elvis Presley movie that had hit town. Shane was our leader, and the undisputed number one Elvis Presley fan.

And speaking of Shane, as I gazed over the low shrubbery that outlined the housing area I saw him coming up Kalihi Street. Shane had a sharp, hands-open-and-to-the-side way of walking. It was so smooth I could already hear the sharpness from afar.

Shane was the one to ask about things you didn't understand; he always knew better. The teachers were stupid enough to put him in the dumb class but we knew that he was the smartest, toughest, coolest, not-to-mention handsomest dude around. We all parted our hair on the side, the way he did. But only he had the privilege (and maybe the kind of hair) to push the front part up and back—Elvis Presley style. Shane had seen all the Elvis movies. The last ones he saw were *G.I. Blues* and *Blue Hawaii*. Shane's favorite color was blue. And so was ours. And it all made perfect sense.

What made Shane look so extra sharp, though, was his pants. We all tried to get our parents to buy us the type of bell-bottom pants—drapes, we called them—that Shane wore. But we didn't know where to buy them. And Shane wouldn't tell us, though I figured out later that his mother made them for him.

Even on J.P.O. duty, he looked so tough, with his square-cut white

71

shirt, his blue drapes, his captain's whistle. Of course, we had voted him captain. Geraldo "Gerry" De la Cruz was lieutenant. Lenny, me, and Gerry, our Gerry, had swept the whole slate by being elected first, second, and third sergeants, respectively. Shane was too cool.

When Shane's features were within sight, when I could see the slight squint he often made when approaching us, a mock sort of sizing up, I greeted him with a quick up-down head motion. He didn't respond.

"Gerry said Elvis Hawaiian," I said the moment Shane was within earshot. He was wearing his customary drapes. And he had on a nifty, blue velour shirt with a string sort of tie at the collar.

"Dass true," Gerry replied.

"Bullshit," Shane said. "He one haole."

"But, but, in *Blue Hawaii* he no look haole. Da buggah brown."

"Dass 'cause dey wen' paint his skin. Dye 'om. Dass what Hollywood do. Dey make 'om look like somet'ing else. Dey can make one haole look Japanee."

"Ey, I no believe you," Gerry said. Shane punched him in the shoulder. "OW! Okay, I believe . . . I believe." Gerry rubbed his arm. "Ow, you fuckah. Sore."

Shane was the smartest guy around.

Then Lenny, always last, arrived. He probably came through Kam Housing, because it seemed like he had come out of nowhere, like he had been hiding in the bushes all the time. When I greeted him, again with a head gesture, a barely perceptible inverted nod, Lenny responded by lifting his eyebrows. No other part of his face moved.

When Lenny had transferred to our school, Kalihi-Kai Elementary, earlier that school year, Shane challenged him to a footrace. When I shouted "MARK! SET! GO!" Lenny ran the wrong way, a route that was perpendicular to Shane's. Together they were like the vectors we were learning about in math class, forming a longer and longer right angle. I laughed till I was blue.

But as I got to know Lenny, I began to suspect that he was smart enough not to show that he could beat Shane . . . yet.

The H.R.T. arrived. We all got on the bus and walked down the aisle to the back so we could look at everybody in front. If anybody turned back to look at us we give that person the stink eye and act tough.

I sat between Shane and Gerry, Shane being on my left. Lenny sat to the left of Shane. We were silent for a minute as the bus sped toward downtown. Then I spoke first.

"So, who is dis Nicky da Cruise Job?"

"You fuckah," Shane said, elbowing my ribs. "You always gotta bring up stupid stuff."

Gerry said, "I t'ink he one, you know, da kine syndicate guy. Like Al Capone . . . Dillinger. . . ."

"Mafia?" I said.

"Yeah."

"Make sense. . . . So we practicing fo' hide from da Mafia. . . ."

Then Shane spoke. "Fucking stupid. You guys so FUCKING STOOPID! He one Russian! He da Russian leadah—"

"How you know?"

"My muddah wen' tell me. He da old bolohead guy."

"Why we gotta hide undah da table 'cause a' one old bolohead guy?" Gerry said. "Why we no jes' beef 'om? If da buggah old."

"Not jes' him," Shane started to say. He sounded pissed. "He get his boys . . . da Russians . . . strong buggahs. . . ."

"What," Gerry said, "dey can beef you?"

"Of course . . . I mean, of course not. Not if one-on-one."

"What if," Gerry said, "what if you take da strongest American guy our age, an' dass pro'bly you, Shane . . . an' you take da strongest Russian guy our age, an' den you guys beef. Who would win?"

I glanced at Lenny. Through all this conversation he had been staring straight ahead, quiet. But when I looked at him he turned to make a mock-serious face at me, then quickly looked straight ahead again.

"Me, of course," Shane said, very serious. "He pro'bly goin' be biggah . . ." He started shadow boxing. ". . . but I no care. . . . I goin' let 'om t'row first, eh. Den I goin' duck. No, no, I goin' give 'om one cross block, den duck an' come up wit' one left uppacut, den hit 'om low, right in the ribs. *OOGH!* Den, if da buggah still standing, I goin' wait fo' he t'row again, duck dis time, turning li' dis . . ." Shane turned his body leftward, toward me, pulling his right arm toward his left shoulder. ". . . den give 'om one . . ." He threw his right hand out toward some shadow enemy, saying ". . . KARATE CHOP IN DA NECK!"

73

Shane took karate lessons; he always reminded us, in case we had forgotten.

"Whoah," Gerry said, as some passengers up front turned to look at us. "Ja' like Tosh Togo." Then he said, "Hey Shane, you can lick one Japanee guy our age who one judo expert? Or kung fu?"

"Tst. . . . Of course. Easy."

We all kept pulling on the cord that rang the bell that announced we were getting off. *BINGBINGBINGBINGBING . . . BINGBINGBINGBINGBING,* to the bus driver's annoyance. We exited then, crossed Smith Street on King, passed a sundry shop, then it was the theater. We each paid our 75 cents for the movie ticket and walked into the snack bar area. We loaded up on popcorn, Pom-poms, M&Ms, Mr. Goodbars, Cokes and 7-Ups. Then we walked into the dark, cavernous escape world just in time for the Looney Tunes.

We took seats way in the back. Me and Gerry, positioning ourselves a seat apart to give ourselves room, sat in the same row. Shane and Lenny, also a seat apart, sat in the row behind us. The good thing about Saturday matinees was that there were always a lot of empty seats.

The warm smells of butter and chocolate wafted through the moviehouse as we began gulping down the goodies and adjusting our eyes to the bright colors of the opening cartoon.

"Hey Gerry. Bugs Bunny look ja'like you."

"Shit, you look like Elmah Fudd. . . . OW! Hey, no kick da chair!"

During the rest of the cartoon, we threw ice and pieces of candy wrappers, kicked chairs, and swore at each other a lot. But we got real quiet when the opening credits to *It Happened At The World's Fair* filled the screen.

The tone for the movie was set early. Elvis and this other guy are in this small plane. They're cropdusters. Elvis—while singing, of course—sparks two nice-looking chicks in a convertible and flies the plane low to check them out.

Then the plot begins to unfold. It turns out that Elvis and his plane-flying partner are saving up all their money so they can start a business of their own. The only problem is that Elvis's partner is a chronic gambler and has already gambled away some of their earnings. So, Elvis has to hide the money and keep it under lock and key.

Elvis, it turns out, is a chronic girl chaser. . . .

"Junk, dis movie. He only like make out wit girls."

"Shaddup, Gerry. Jes' watch."

Elvis's partner somehow gets hold of the money, about four hundred dollars, finds a poker game to join into, and proceeds to lose everything and more. By the time Elvis discovers that the money is missing and finds the location of the poker game — this is after he has been chased with a gun by the father of a girl he is caught making out with — his partner owes the rest of the players seven hundred dollars. Elvis accuses the other players of cheating him, suggesting that they were doing something under the table, and a fight ensues.

"All right."

"Wow. You saw dat? He wen' kick 'om."

"Of course. Elvis know karate."

"Whoa, watch him smoke da guys."

"Wow. You saw dat? You saw dat? Karate chop?"

"Wheah?"

"You blind mullet —"

Elvis was fighting about a half-dozen guys, licking them all, while his partner struggled to fight one.

"Dere. He doin' 'om again."

"Shhhh."

Elvis grabs his friend and they haul ass out of town. The timing is perfect. A pickup truck, driven by a Chinese man, the passenger his little daughter, stops and picks them up.

"Look like your faddah, Gerry."

"Shaddap."

"Look like your sistah, Gerry."

"Fuck you. You cannot tell da difference between one Japanee and one —"

"Shhhhh!"

"What you said, Gerry? Elvis Hawaiian?"

"Shaddap."

"She your speed, Gerry."

"Shaddap. She *your* speed. An' you bettah not kick my chair."

"Shhhhhhh!"

I noticed that Elvis's hair was combed back even more so than I had remembered. And it looked real shiny, like he loaded it up with some kind of hair oil. It looked kind of funny to me. I figured that Shane was going to start using more pomade.

The Chinese guy and his daughter—she introduces herself as Sue Lin; Elvis says he is Mike; she calls him Mr. Mike—are heading out toward Seattle to see the World's Fair. Sue Lin's father tells Elvis and his partner they are welcome to head up there with them. They think it's a great idea.

But when they reach the fair, something goes wrong. The girl's father, who runs a produce business, discovers he has to make an important delivery, and won't be able to take his daughter to the fair as promised. Elvis, of course, saves the day by volunteering to take the little girl around while his partner goes off to find them work. "Mr. Mike" and Sue Lin check out the Space Needle, the Dream Car—a futuristic vehicle (more than a few "ooh's" and "wow's" from the movie audience)—, and they eat a lot of junk food. Sue Lin ends up having an awful bellyache, and Elvis takes her to the dispensary. Of course, Elvis falls for the nurse. . . .

"Getting stale again. When dey goin' fight again? Hey, Shane, no t'row ice."

"Yeah," I said, "no t'row ice. Who t'rowing ice?"

Elvis spends the rest of the movie chasing after the nurse, and sings enough songs to fill an album. His partner continues to gamble, but he also gets them a potentially lucrative job delivering some goods in their plane across the Canadian border. It turns out, though, that it's a gun-smuggling operation involving some syndicate type. Elvis reneges on the deal, which leads to a film-ending fight that almost makes the movie worthwhile.

When we got out of the theater no one said anything for several minutes. We walked sort of absently in the same direction —down Fort Street—and reacquainted ourselves with the overwhelming brightness of the sky and the sunlit street.

Gerry spoke first: "Wow, I like da way Elvis wen' smoke da guys. Ten of 'om against him."

"Was mo' like five," I said.

"Seven," Shane said. No one disputed that.

"Silly eh," Lenny said, "da way everytime Elvis sing get all kine music backup—like all da musicians stay in da bushes o' somet'ing." Then Lenny started singing, doing a mock Elvis. "Happy ending, happy ending/Give me a story with a *boom* happy end—"

"Tst," Shane said, interrupting Lenny's performance, "dass jes' Hollywood."

"Hey," Gerry said. "We go see *Gunfight At O.K. Corral*. Stay showing at Hawaii Teatah. I bet get mo' action."

"We no mo' nuff money," Shane said. "Unless you goin' treat us."

"Oh, yeah . . ." Gerry said, as if remembering, "we no mo' nuff money."

"Tired, cowboy pictures, anyway. Get nuff a' dat on T.V."

"Hey," Gerry quickly added, "anybody saw *Stoney Burke* las' night? Stoney wen fall off his horse and—"

"I saw," Shane said. "Was junk."

"Was *good*." POOM. "OW! Okay, was junk den."

We walked past Metronome music store. We saw some guys testing out some electric guitars. A couple of them were so good that they were even practicing their steps.

"Wow," Lenny said. "Maybe dey play fo' da Spiedels."

"Da guys who play 'Pipeline'?" I asked.

"No . . . 'Telstar.'" Lenny turned and grinned at me. I grinned back. We walked on till Lenny said, "Hey, we go beach. Still early."

"Nah," Shane said. "I no like get my pants dirty. Besides, we no mo' towels."

"No need towels fo' dry off," Lenny said. "And pants . . . can wash."

"Yeah, we go," Gerry chimed.

"Yeah," I said.

Shane didn't seem to like the idea. He didn't seem to like being challenged, but for once he was outnumbered. His jaw seemed to tighten. "Okay, shit. We go den."

We always wore swimming trunks underneath our pants. It's a habit you learn quick enough when you grow up in a hot, tropical climate. The first time Lenny went out with us, though, he hadn't been all that acclimated. He only had B.V.D.'s on underneath, so we couldn't go to Waikiki or Ala Moana. We ended up swimming bareballs at Sand Island.

77

It took us about a half hour to get to Ala Moana beach. We were all hot and sweaty by then, and anxious to swim out to the reef that functioned as a breakwater. We laid our clothes on the sand, Shane folding his carefully, and jumped in. We swam to the reef, took some dives off the rocks, shoved each other's heads in, then swam back to the shore. Then, using a scrunched up paper cup with a little bit of sand in it, we played Hawaiian-style football in the shallow water till the game got out of hand with everybody stretching the already loose rules more and more. Finally, we got out.

By then we were all both hungry and thirsty. We knew, however, that if we ate or drank something we'd be using our bus fare home. Still, it seemed like it would be worth it. We checked to see how much money we had. Shane had fifty-three cents. I had thirty-five. Lenny had thirty-five also. Gerry, from his vast array of pockets, pulled out two long combs, a short one, a piece of string he identified as belonging to a yoyo, his ticket stub, but only managed to scrape up twenty-three cents. Together we had enough for hotdogs and soft drinks. That's about it.

"I tot you said you wanted fo' see *Gunfight At O.K. Corral?*" Shane said to Gerry as he handed him twelve cents. You mo' broke dan us."

"I tot I had . . . I fo'got." Shane karate-chopped him in the neck. "OW! Fucking Shane, why you always gotta whack *me*? Whack dem . . ." Gerry looked toward me and Lenny ". . . sometime." Shane responded by giving Gerry a headlock.

We bought our cokes and hotdogs at the Ala Moana Beach Ewa concession and devoured the food and drink in what seemed like seconds. Still, it was great. Then we started walking through one of the woodier areas of the park to get on with the long trek home.

Then, from out of nowhere, we heard an Elvis Presley song:
She wrote upon it
Return to sender, address unknown
No such number, no such zone . . .
We were all suddenly reeling, spinning slowly around in a small clearing, grinning, goofy-like, wondering where the music was coming from. "Whoa," Lenny said, "ja'like in da movie." Shane started doing a mock-Elvis routine, moving his legs to and fro.

Then out of the green, it seemed, two big guys approached us. They looked to be eighth graders, at least.

What are movies without bad guys? These guys looked like they'd fit the bill.

"Hey," the Japanese-looking guy said to Shane, "How much money you get?" His companion turned his transistor radio down.

"Not-t'ing," Shane said.

"What about you, Japanee?" He was glaring at Gerry.

"Not-t'ing," Shane said again.

"Hey, I talking to you, Potagee? I not talking to you."

Gerry dug into one of the many pockets of his jeans, and, like he knew the exact location, pulled out a dollar bill and handed it to the hijacker. Shane, Lenny, and me all looked at Gerry, startled; he did not look at us. Then the hijacker looked at Lenny and me, but before he could utter a word we both pulled our pockets out to show that we had nothing. Then his attention turned again to Shane. "You get nice clothes. You must get money—"

"I no mo'," Shane said, looking down at the dirt.

"Eh, leave 'om alone, Russ," the hijacker's Portuguese-looking companion said. "Dey already gave us. If he said he no mo', he no mo'."

I calculated that Shane must have had six cents somewhere on him. Why didn't he just give it?

"Eh," the guy named Russ said, "but I t'ink dis guy t'ink he hot shit." Russ glared at Shane. His pupils seemed dilated. His eyes were red, but also a bit yellowy. "You hot shit?"

Shane looked down. "No," he said, quick but soft.

"Look at me when you talk."

"Leave 'om alone, Russ." His partner pulled at Russ's arm. Russ pulled his arm back.

"Use your karate, Shane," Gerry whispered.

"What?" Russ said, feigning surprise. "Dis panty know karate?"

"Yeah," Gerry said. "He can break your ass." Shane glared at Gerry.

"Oh boy, I scared now. Dis guy know ka-ra-te." Russ went into a fake, exaggerated karate position. "YAHT-YAHT-YAHT!" he yelled, throwing awkward blows in the direction of Shane. "Come on. Break my ass."

"Yeah, break his ass already," his companion said. He seemed exasperated.

"You goin' break my ass?" Russ said, taunting Shane.

Shane looked at the dirt on the ground. "No."

"How come? You one panty? One karate panty?" Shane glanced up. He saw our eyes on him. There was a pause. "Come on! Talk!"

"Come on, Russ. Let's go. We already get dere money."

"Yeah, but . . . dey have clothes. Look at dis nice shirt." Russ grabbed at Shane's shirt. Shane pushed his hand away. Russ responded by bunching up Shane's shirt collar, and pulling Shane closer. Shane pulled away. The shirt tore.

"You fuckah . . . ma muddah wen'—"

"Your mom-mee? Baby needs his mom-mee?" Russ kicked dirt on Shane's khaki drapes. Shane dusted it off. Russ then rubbed his slipper bottom on it. Shane shoved him away. Russ lost his cool. "You fuckah," Russ said, and he threw a long, roundhouse right that smashed into Shane's left ear. I grimaced as I heard the crunch.

"OW! My ear! You fuckah!" Shane started crying. He bent low, cupping his ear, tears streaming down his face. "You cheat, you fuckah. You punch in da ear! OW-WEE. . . ."

Before Russ could react, Lenny charged the much larger guy, catching him off-balance. Lenny threw wild but lightning quick punches at Russ, who probably could have killed Lenny, if Lenny would only let him swing back, let alone breathe, against the flurry of his small blows.

The other big kid moved slightly, like he thought about jumping in. Gerry and I moved correspondingly, to let him know we'd jump in too. He stopped, held a hand up, indicating a momentary truce. "It's cool," he said, with exaggerated nods. "Let 'om fight."

Shane was still bent low, almost in squatting position, holding his ear. He kept crying out "Cheat, cheat, da fuckah punch ear."

Then Russ fell down, more from being off-balance, it seemed. Lenny kept swinging at him. "You fucking Russ," his friend said, "you let one small guy lick you."

"Okay, nuff," Russ began to say, "nuff already. I sorry. I nevah mean fo' cheat, okay?"

Lenny finally got off him. Slowly, Russ stood up, holding his nose, which was bleeding steadily. He also had a black eye.

"Shit," his friend said. "Now I gotta wash you up. How embarrassing." Oblivious to us, he led Russ away. Then he stopped for a second, turned up his radio, then off they continued, disappearing in the same bushes that they seemed to materialize out of. We were left with a wounded Shane and the fading sounds of the transistor radio:

> . . . and before that, that was the King himself singing
> his hit song from the movie, Girls, Girls, Girls . . . you're
> listening to the number one station (female voices:)
> K-P-O-I—Honolulu . . . .

As soon as Russ and his companion were gone Gerry shouted "Hey, look!" and pointed to a dollar bill right where the scuffle had occurred. It must have been the dollar that Gerry had given to Russ. It must have fallen out of his pocket. Gerry ran to retrieve it. Lenny went up to him and punched his arm.

"You fuckah. You nevah tell us you had dat much."

"I fo'got . . . fo' real, I fo'got."

"Yeah . . . sure."

"Hey, I treat you guys, okay? I pay fo' everybody's bus fare."

"You fuckah. You bettah buy us Cokes too."

"Yeah, yeah. But fo' real . . . I fo'got."

We had washed Shane up at Ala Moana Shopping Center, then had hiked up on Keeaumoku Street to King to catch the 1R Kalihi bus home.

We didn't sit in the back. In fact, we sat way up front, right behind the driver. Me and Lenny sat together; Shane and Gerry sat behind us. Shane kept telling Gerry, "If da buggah nevah cheat, man . . . I woulda use' my karate," and Gerry would be saying, "Yeah, you woulda killed 'om, Shane. Fucking cheatah."

The downtown stores like Long's Drugs and Woolworth's, a dizzying blur from inside the speeding bus, cast their large shadows in the late afternoon. The places we had been but hours before, though it seemed like months, were history. Shane said, "An' dis panty," referring to Lenny, "he no can even beef. He cannot fight fo' shit. You saw how he swing?" Shane imitated Lenny's wild blows in exaggerated style. I saw Lenny's fists tighten on his lap. Shane and Gerry went on talking.

"Wow, your pants all had it," Gerry said.

"Yeah. Ma muddah goin' kill me. Shit."

"Da fuckah cheat. He mo' worse dan da Russians," Gerry said, his voice trailing off.

"You had money," Lenny said suddenly, turning to punch Gerry in the arm. "Fucking stashah."

"Yeah, stashah," I echoed. Then it got silent and uncomfortable for a while. It wasn't till we were way past Aala Park and nearing Palama Theater that Shane broke the ice.

"An' da buggah call me 'Potagee,'" he said. "I only part. I get Hawaiian . . . English . . . some Chinese. . . ."

"Yeah, you get everything, Shane," Lenny cut in. I could not really tell if he were being straightforward or sarcastic then, sarcasm being pretty new to me. In fact, I think it was Lenny who started introducing such nuances to my ears.

Still, for the most part, edges were being lost in translation. Nicky da Cruise, Job or Chef. Who is the guy? Were we hearing it right? I mean, you'd like to know who's threatening you . . . and why. I glanced at Lenny. And as I caught his conspiratorial smile I was under the table again.

May 1969 — A moment later

Lenny's eyes again moved in the direction of Lynette Toma's crotch. This time my eyes followed. I had hoped he hadn't summoned me under the table to play spark-panty. We hadn't done that in ages. Just the thought of it, made me hot with embarrassment — yet curious.

And there it was, Lynette's crotch, jiggling like Jello. Usually, all the girls wore bikini bottoms because dresses and skirts were so short in those days. Few were ever brave enough to wear panties. Lynette's legs were going 280; she always had that leg-shaking habit. At the moment she was busy talking to Jolene Kauhane, another fox, and they seemed to have no idea that me and Lenny were under.

Lenny and I grinned at each other. I figured we'd get caught — but it was worth it. At that moment I thought Lynette was the foxiest girl in the world.

Then she covered it up — probably her sixth sense. It always happened like that; such moments were so brief. Then I looked at

Lenny and whispered (though not as soft as before), "So who is this guy, Nicky da Cruise Job?" and we both started laughing.

The laughing seemed to reverberate off of every conceivable wall. Suddenly, the whole class's attention was turned to Lenny and me, the two idiots under the table. Then Lenny came out from under and started yelling, "BWAAAAAAAAAAAAAHHHHH . . . AIR RAID . . . AIR RAID . . . ALL UNITS ON ALERT . . . THIS IS NOT, I REPEAT, THIS IS *NOT* A FALSE ALARM . . . WE *ARE* BEING ATTACKED BY THE SOVIETS . . . THEY ARE ABOUT TO . . . BURY US . . . UNDER THE TABLE, EVERYONE. . . ."

Lenny was diverting all the attention away from me.
He jumped on tables, made siren noises — school was never able to stifle Lenny, the way it did so many of us; it would take a lot more than that.

"I tell you, boys are such —" I heard Lynette start to whisper to Jolene. I couldn't believe it. Their whispers seemed so loud from under the table. It seemed as if I were in an adjacent room from the one they were in, and their room was being bugged. It was as if I wore headphones — like I had seen on T.V. — and was suddenly in on their innermost secrets.

But then I heard "Da teachah coming, da teachah coming," our very own air-raid warning. A very effective one. In an instant the class was tellingly silent, a world of deaf-mutes. Marsha, the monitor, sat casually in her place at the teacher's desk up front. Somebody's hand tossed a paper plane under the table and it hit my arm. Another piece of paper fell to the floor and a girl's foot kicked it more under.

It was too late for me to come out from under the table without getting nabbed. Yet if I didn't come out, the teacher would notice I was missing. I thought of how often I seemed to be caught in similar dilemmas.

Strangely enough, Mrs. Harada went through the routine of collecting test papers without noting my absence. Someone had probably stuck my paper under his or hers, and got my paper handed in. As a class we were good at covering up for each other.

I cherished my newly discovered invisibility — something I thought only Hollywood could do.

Then the bell rang. I stayed there through the shuffle. At one point, Lenny ducked his head under. "Somattah?" he said. "Catch da stre—hey, you all right?" I waved him away. He understood. I made no move to go to math class. Instead, I thought of vectors. I thought of how we all seemed to start at the same place and then grow further and further apart. And I don't just mean those infinitesimal misunderstandings that grow into disputes of global proportions. I'm just talking about growing up. I mean, what's so great about growing up if you keep losing friends?

So what if Shane didn't know karate, at least not to the extent that he claimed. So what if Gerry stashed bucks sometimes. So what if I knew Lenny for a couple of years before I found out he lived in that housing project and didn't want to let on how poor he thought his family was, not appreciating for a long time that the rest of us weren't much better off, or that it didn't matter. Shane and Gerry had already been lost in the shuffle, lost in those trying transitions to intermediate and high school. Now me and Lenny were going to part ways. We, like so many others our age, had received draft notices. I was escaping to college; Lenny was headed for Nam. He didn't want to go. But more important, he didn't want to not go. He had too much pride.

Lenny was going to Nam because some men in nice suits in Paris couldn't agree on the size and shape of their negotiating table.

Lenny was going to Nam as part of Richard Nixon's *Vietnamization* program.

And it made me sad.

It made me less sad, though, to remember Lenny singing the song that Elvis sang at the end of *It Happened At The World's Fair:*

Happy ending, happy ending
Give me a story with a (boom) *happy ending . . .*

though it just so happens that the world—except in movies, maybe—is not fair. Because I still wanted to believe in happy endings.

I wanted to bask in the wet-dream world of Jellolike crotches, in dark, cavernous theaters, living out Hollywood scenes . . . where background music is there for you whenever you want to sing, where fights work out as planned, where the bad guys always lose. . . .

But now I didn't even know who the bad guys were.

I wanted to lash out at my shadow enemy. No, not Nicky da Cruise Job, or Khrushchev, or cruise missiles, but the part of me that is torn, ripped apart, like my drafts of love notes to Lynette, like my draft notice, the part that won't let me come up from under the table.

Daybreak Over Haleakala/Heartbreak Memories
(A Two-Sided Hit)

"Are you asleep?"

A few seconds of silence. Then: "Yeah. You must be too."

Bud and I giggled like two children cheating on nap time. "Well," I said as I sat up in my sleeping bag, "no use lying around." Bud got up too. I gazed at the long row of sleeping bags stretched out across the sands of Hakioawa. It dawned on me at that moment that Bud and I were probably the only souls awake on the island.

He lit a cigarette and offered me one. I didn't smoke but I accepted. It seemed right. As I flicked ashes on the sand the moon appeared. I imagine Bud was watching too. He sat silent.

Crescent-shaped—the heart of it implied—the moon had risen gloriously over Haleakala, the house of the sun, over on the island of Maui. The ocean, the sand, the rocks along the shore, everything—shimmered.

"Beautiful," Bud said. I nodded. "So nice."

"Yeah."

"Too bad I gotta piss so fucking *bad!*"

Those words caused me to choke on my smoke. While I tried to suppress both my laughter and my choke-induced cough, to not disturb the others, Bud made gestures that suggested anguish, squeezing his legs together just to soak me for more painful laughter. All the while I thought: Here we are on a serious journey to an island that is being bombed to dust and still we are being hopelessly irreverent. *Buddy boy,* I said to myself as the coughs subsided, *you'll never change.*

"Here," I said finally. "Use my flashlight."

"And go alone?"

As we walked slowly in our bare feet toward the kiawe thicket, carefully avoiding thorns, I found myself amused (and, to tell the truth, relieved) that this powerfully built University of Hawaii football player, a first-string linebacker who was often cited for his ferocity on the playing field, was afraid to walk into the bushes alone. But being on the island of Kahoolawe did that kind of thing to you. Uninhabited as it was supposed to be, you couldn't help but wonder what lurked about.

We had been drawn to the "target island," the smallest in the Hawaiian island chain, on what was called an access trip by a mutual friend, Kaeo Perkins. Like Bud, Kaeo played football for the UH. And he and I shared a journalism class. Kaeo was also a member of the Protect Kahoolawe Ohana, or PKO, a Hawaiian activist group who had fought the United States Navy in an effort to wrest control of the island from military hands and their alleged abuses — that is, bombing it for target practice (in case, Kaeo would say, the United States ever got attacked by an island). As Bud and I pulled up our shorts (I found I had to piss, too) and started back toward our sleeping bags, I recalled reading somewhere that when Hawaiian activists — nine of them — first landed on Kahoolawe in 1976, all but two were quickly picked up by the U.S. Coast Guard. The two who stayed were not seen because (ahem) they had gone into the thicket to relieve themselves.

Back in our sleeping bags, we lay staring at the pre-dawn sky.

"Ever notice how the unseen part of the moon blends with the sky?" Bud asked.

"Hmmm . . . yeah, know?" I wondered why I never seem to notice the obvious.

Knowing Bud, I also waited for the punch line. Or a discourse on the moon . . . and the stars . . . and black holes and white dwarfs and on and on. Bud was an astronomy major — an unlikely field for a jock — and often let us know. But all he said was, "the reason is . . . ah, forget it. It's just nice." Then he faded to sleep.

I felt like the only person alive in the universe.

I think it was raining that spring morning when the subject of Kahoolawe came up. I had met Bud and Kaeo for coffee at the University of Hawaii's Campus Center cafeteria. It was midterm time, semicidal burnout time, and the three of us — and a disjointed parade of others — retreated to "the caf" between classes for quick coffee fixes. Caf*fiends,* we called ourselves.

"But, like, what's there to see?" Bud was saying as I sat down on a cold seat. "Just one rock."

"Bud, you fricken babozo," Kaeo replied. "It's like any adda island. Like Maui, Kauai . . ."

"Oh, yeah, get hotels . . . rent a cars . . ."

"No. Jes' get da bes' beaches. Good surf, even . . . and no mo' traffic."

"Surf? How big?"

"Biggah dan you . . . at least three-to-four."

"Three to four . . .?" Bud put his head down. "Shit, I just blew a fucking midterm." He looked up, looking somewhat serious for a change. "Three to four, eh? You better be right, Kaeo . . . 'cause I'm going."

Bud Newman was an avid — forget avid — obsessive body surfer, as are many who are raised in the Hawaiian Islands. He was a Hawaii-born haole who had hard blue eyes and dark brown, slightly wavy hair which he always covered with a green UH baseball cap. Bud also had a passion for rock and roll — Stones, Springsteen, Seger, and those are just ones that start with an "S." Kaeo was part-Hawaiian yet full-on into the culture. Though he spoke English as well as anybody, Kaeo usually opted for his comfy pidgin. He wore wire-rimmed glasses which shaded his green eyes. And though he was as muscular as Bud, he was leaner.

Kaeo looked at his watch. "Get time fo' one mo' cup." He stood up, pulled Bud's cap off and put it on his head as he went for a refill. Bud swore at him. When he returned he addressed me: "Hey, why you no come too? You should write about da place. You can write."

"Bullshit."

"Just do 'om fo' da course."

"For my *term* paper?"

"Yeah . . . jes' tell da prof you goin' write about what it's like to go to Kahoolawe." Kaeo held up an invisible frame with his hands. "The Kahoolawe Experience."

"Why *you* no do dat." There went *my* English.

"I did, twice, last year. In fact," Kaeo now spoke in a whisper,

88

"I used da same pepah *twice*. And got A's both times."

"So," Bud interjected, "lend him *that* paper."

"Yeah. Lend me *that* paper."

"Not till I use 'om again."

"Nah, come on, go," Bud said, grabbing my shoulder. "I don't want to be the only new guy there."

"See," Kaeo jumped in. "You gotta come."

But they weren't convincing me. And they gave up trying. Minutes later, when Kaeo was leaving, he told Bud, teasingly: "Da t'ing about the island, boy, is dat nobody comes back da same."

"Yeah, I notice you comb your hair different now."

Still teasing: "You'll see."

I don't know if I was just bored with school, or just burnt out, or what, but I found myself muttering, "What if I go?"

"What you mean 'what if,' brah?" Kaeo quickly replied. "I putting yo' name down." I sat back, took a deep breath, then knocked Bud's hat off Kaeo's head.

The access had been scheduled for the last week of March, during the latter part of spring break. Bud and Kaeo would be through with spring practice and I couldn't come up with any excuses to get me out of going. Instead I forced the situation upon myself by promising my journalism prof a paper. Part of the deal was I could miss class the following Monday. The Sunday we'd return would be my birthday, and I figured I'd deserve a day off.

Bud and I had to attend an orientation session — mandatory for first timers. A woman named Susan conducted the session. She was a tall, part-Hawaiian woman whose beauty kind of crept up on you. She was well-tanned, with waist-length black hair. And when she smiled she lit up the dingy YWCA room reserved for the occasion.

Sue gave us newcomers the rundown on the kinds of supplies the PKO recommended we bring: collapsible jugs to fill up at Maalaea Harbor on Maui — for there is no running water on Kahoolawe; waterproof flashlights — waterproof everything, if possible; fisherman's tabis — the best footwear to deal with the kiawe thorns as well as to get a grip on things; but no booze or pakalolo — leave that stuff on Maui.

Then we had to sign forms releasing the Navy from liability

in case any one of us blew up in a million pieces.

After that we viewed some slides that allowed Sue to show as well as explain how the island had been devastated by the bombing once the goats ate up all the vegetation. How the goats got into the picture I didn't know, because I was focusing more on the conveyer of the information. Bud must have been tuned into the same wavelength. When Sue asked if there were any questions, he said, "Are you going?"

"Yes, I am," Sue replied.

"Good," Bud said. "'Cause I need somebody to show me the archaeological sites . . . or whatevers." There were rumblings of laughter all around.

Finally Sue talked about *ukanas,* Hawaiian for luggage, I presumed, and how we would be brought to the island on a boat that literally dropped us off—into the water—fifty to a hundred yards offshore. "Make sure everything you bring is wrapped in at least three layers of garbage bags—the 3 mils thick size—'cause *ev*erything goes in the water. *Ev*erything . . . cameras and other expensive equipment have been ruined because they got wet."

That night marked the first time Bud and I were together without Kaeo. Kaeo had told us he wouldn't come because, as he put it, "*I* don't need orientation." It turned out interesting. Like a couple of sailors on shore leave before sailing, we took on the city of Honolulu. Cruising in Bud's silver-blue Mazda *RX-7,* we obliterated joints while Bud continuously fed his tape deck with songs he wanted to turn me on to. And in between the short, frenzied drives there were stops at various bars and other night spots for equally frenetic moments and quick beers. Bars and joints, bars and joints . . .

And tapes. Bud had cassette tapes for every reason, season, rhyme and time of day dispersed throughout the car—in the glove compartment, under the seats, on the dashboard, next to the handbrake—Police, Doors, REM, Pink Floyd, Elvis Costello, you name it. With Bud shifting gears and switching tapes like an FM deejay we coasted on the H-1 to "San Lorenzo," blitzed down University Avenue to the feverish strains of "Layla," reggaed to Bob Marley on Kalakaua Avenue . . .

During the David Bowie song, "Changes," which we screamed along to *(Ch-ch-ch-changes . . . Turn and face the strange),* when we were wasted to the point that Bud's driving was affected, Bud said, "*Change.* You think we're gonna change?"

"Shit. Everything changes. We all change . . . even the light. Bud. I said the light. The *light* just changed."

"Oh."

All that evening Bud drove recklessly, often causing me to press imaginary brake pedals from my position in the "death seat," as well as shout Kaeo's favorite line, "Bud, you fricken babozo," around scary turns. But something happened that changed his driving style to slow and deliberate, something immediately sobering.

On the corner of Kapiolani Boulevard and McCully, there appeared to be a roadblock. Bud quickly slowed down and sprayed his mouth with breath freshener. As we neared the scene we saw the ambulance . . . police cars . . . a tow truck . . . a badly smashed late model Toyota *Celica.* One man lay on the ground. He was being attended to by medics who were placing him on a stretcher. Another man, the driver, was pinned in his seat in the upside-down car. People were trying to free him. He wasn't moving. As Bud drove me home I'm sure he was thinking what I was thinking: *It could have been us.*

Suddenly, Kahoolawe loomed as a much safer place.

Change, we are going to change. That became the big joke. But as I lay awake on Hakioawa sands, gazing at the first rays of sun, it was already clear to me that Bud was not his usual self. He seemed somewhat subdued. Except for our brief episode on the beach earlier, I hadn't heard a wise remark from him since we had landed.

Still I had no doubt that this was temporary, that once we had returned to Oahu, Bud Newman would be his old self again.

The sun had begun to ascend over Haleakala, hot on the trail of the fading moon. I had thought that the daybreak I had witnessed twenty-four hours earlier at Maalaea was breathtaking, with its deep pink and orange glow edging over the verdigris and into the soft blue. But from Kahoolawe . . . the lights over on Makena — tiny rectangles of blue and orange — were still visible. Seven miles away it looked like Sleepytown. Then the ocean, from periphery to periphery, burst into color — rippling waves of orange-lavender melding and bending over into this blue and that blue in gold and silvery light. Those sleeping on the beach began getting up from their refreshing slumbers like clockwork. Or like mercury lamps in reverse. I stood up and stretched too, and began folding my sleeping bag as the others did. After everyone had gone to wash up or to the cooking area I nudged Bud a few times. "Hey, Bud, get up. Beautiful morning."

"Eh, come on . . . I just fell asleep . . ." He turned over. ". . . have mercy."

After nudging him a few more times and listening to his moans, I began my tired trudge away from him to join the others. At one point I turned around and looked at him — the only object on the entire beach. He had his cap on, and was sewed up in his sleeping bag. A funny sight — if it weren't so corpselike.

On the way to the island, Bud kept ribbing Kaeo.

"Okay, get surf . . . and sand . . . but like, ah, what's there to *see?*"

"Lotta t'ings. Bettah dan Disneyland."

"Oh. You mean . . ." Bud snickered. ". . . the damage." Kaeo grabbed him by the shorts and made like he would throw Bud overboard.

The *Constellation,* a seaworthy craft with a skyworthy name, skipped past Molokini, a crescent-shaped atoll, obverse to the silvery moon above. I began to feel ill from the diesel fumes and sought out a section of the boat where I could find relief. At one point I leaned over the edge to feel the spray and to fill my lungs with fresh air.

"Hey. No jump yet." I recognized the voice. It was Susan.

"Oh. Hi." I felt stupid.

"Howzit. . . . Better in the front, you know. Less sway."

"I'll be all right." Sue smiled, then headed toward the bow. I went back to see where Bud and Kaeo were. I found them in the pilothouse, still going at it.

"Looks like a rock to me," Bud was saying to Kaeo. The "rock" turned out to be a pretty large island.

"I gon' rock you, man," Kaeo replied. Then he turned to me. "No get your pepah wet, eh? Lots to write about."

"I forgot my pen."

"I get. Pepahmate, Bic, Flair, whatevah you like. Black ink, blue ink, red, orange . . ." I covered my ears and backed away. "Green ink, purple . . ."

Minutes later it was "JUMP!"

We had gone from the *Constellation* to the small, maneuverable craft that was called a *zodiac*. I thought it would be easy. Wrong. Fifty yards out, we were told to jump, and everything and everyone but the steersman went overboard. There was about thirty-five of us. We threw the *ukanas,* the plastic water jugs, and ourselves into the water.

So there we were, pushing our luggage in, trying to time our thrusts to flow with the three foot (and surfable) waves. I guess it hit me then that there'd be no room service.

Ashore, we dragged everything and everyone in.

Slowly, we settled in. We unpacked our *ukanas,* reserved our camping spots, hung out to dry the things that, in spite of the garbage bag wrappings, still got wet. Wet clothes. Wet paperbacks. We ate some of Kaeo's soggy cookies . . .

Instead of exploring the shoreline like the rest of us new-comers, Bud chose to stay at the base camp at Hakioawa with Kaeo and the regulars who worked either on the traditional *hale* — a planned meeting house; the hula mound — to be used for traditional dancing and other cultural ceremonies; and the garden of indigenous plants. These were all symbols of the Protect Kahoolawe Ohana's efforts to make valid their claim of a Hawaiian resettlement of the island.

After I got used to the feeling of kiawe thorns accumulating on the underpart of my slippers (I chose not to try the tabis yet), I walked alone along the shore. We had been instructed to not stray inland and to watch out for unfired shells.

I loved it immediately. Charcoal-grey sands sparkled even in daylight. I was intrigued by the sparse kiawe, the smooth stones, the claylike, crumbling rock. The solitude.

When we gathered together early that evening for dinner, we were first treated to a lecture by military personnel, an officer and two Explosive Ordnance Disposal (EOD) experts on the dangers of picking up anything that looked like it could blow up

93

in your face.

Then we gathered to *pule*. We prayed standing in a circle, holding hands. And then we ate. Afterwards, some of the people hit the hammocks to get a jump on the next day. Others, Kaeo, Bud, and me included, sat or stood around the kiawe wood campfire and told or listened to stories till way past midnight.

It had been Kaeo's suggestion that we rough it with about two dozen others on the beach. It sounded like a good idea then, but the next morning . . . my back and head ached. I had been awake the entire night, and the exhaustion I felt made it hard to be cooperative and helpful "ohana style," which was defined by Noa Kekipi, a PKO member, as "if you see dirty dishes, you clean them."

I did manage to clean some dishes — in pots of varying-degrees-of-clean rinsing water, and later washed these same pots in the tide pools. I also helped gather kiawe for charcoal fire, hoping at times that somebody would tell me to take a break. But everyone was too busy to notice.

Everyone except Bud was up and about, and plans were made to take us newcomers on a hike to the top of the island, a spot called *Moa'ula iki*. Sandwiches and drinks were packed and we were told to be ready at ten a.m. sharp for an all-day hike.

Before we left, I tried a few more times to awaken Bud, without success. I even mentioned that Susan was leading us on a tour of the "archaeological sites or whatevers" and it only elicited a "leave-me-alone" groan. So off we went without him.

Sue and I walked side by side for a good part of the trek. Apparently, she had heard that I was writing an article or something — this "writer" business was getting out of hand — and made the extra effort to sort of "be there" as someone who could explicate things for me along the way.

There was little she needed to say; it was all there to see. Much of the island was stark, barren, just as one would imagine. The red, hard-packed ground — top soil all gone — ran aslant for miles, it seemed, in every direction. The little vegetation we saw was usually found in the gullies, especially those that were washed out into ravines. Occasionally, we'd find projectiles about two inches long, and sometimes we'd see in the smoothed surfaces of rocks, and on the claylike, polished edges of harsh slopes, an array

94

of colors. This was caused by smooth cylindrical objects scraping against them—objects like missiles.

At one point we came across a dead goat. It was an adult male and had been dead for just a few days. Flies were all over its head, and we didn't want to get too close. We did get close enough to find it had been killed by gunshot.

It had been dry and hot for most the trip, but when we neared the top we were suddenly treated to cool, steady winds. And just as suddenly there were hundreds of trees, a wispy, willowy sort I didn't recognize that leaned almost horizontal in the wind. Sue told me that the Navy had agreed to plant them in compliance with a court action and after some negotiating sessions with the PKO. The Navy had also agreed to eradicate the goat population. The success or failure of the U.S. Navy in these matters was debatable . . . and debated.

At the top we formed a circle and prayed. Then, like pilgrims at the designated shrine after a hard journey, we each wanted our quiet moment and either stood in the *pali* wind or sat on a rock or wandered about. Everyone seemed taken by the view, a lei of islands and mountains—Lanai, Molokai, West Maui Mountains, Haleakala—that seemed to surround the target island. Like they did, I'm sure, I experienced moments of cutting serenity.

At the topmost point of the island there were two boulder-sized slabs of rock. One lay atop the other. And one could only speculate as to how the gigantic slabs got up there. Sue told those of us standing around that these slabs were a communication device that ancient Hawaiians used to relay messages across the channel. She said that a *kahuna,* a priest, would strike the top slab with a hammerlike object and chant. She pointed to a long, straight crack on the top slab. The crack, she said, pointed a straight line to a similar set-up many miles away on Molokai, where the message would be received and sometimes relayed. Other times it would originate there and go the other way. I didn't believe all this . . . but I didn't doubt it either.

As we headed back I felt somewhat moved, yet cautiously distanced in a way that made me feel sure that a Bruce Springsteen concert would more likely change me than Kahoolawe would.

Still, I couldn't wait to tell Bud what he had missed . . . and what I had seen.

When we returned, Noa came up to me. He said Bud had "flipped out" and had to be *medevac'd* to Maui.

"What do you mean, 'flipped out?'" I bit real hard on the corner of my lip.

"He just . . . couldn't handle. He got emotionally distraught."

"What . . .? How . . .?"

"I'm not sure what happened. He and Kaeo were together. Kaeo was showing him some *heiaus,* and I guess they came across some petroglyphs, some that even the archaeologists hadn't come across . . . I guess . . . Man, he must be on some kind of guilt trip."

"Is he going to be all right?" None of this made any sense to me. I left a sleeping Bud, and returned to some kind of madness.

"Oh, yeah. He'll be all right." Noa took a deep drag from a cigarette. "He's not the first . . . well, now the Navy's got another excuse for us not coming here . . . too many Hawaiians flipping out. Fucking assholes . . . . But how the fuck are we supposed to react?" He took another deep drag then flicked his cigarette down and mashed it into the sand.

"It's weird, though," I said, "'cause Bud's not Hawaiian . . ."

"What do you mean, he's not Hawaiian?"

"I mean . . . I know he was born here and all that . . ."

Noa looked at me like I was an idiot. "What do you mean he's not Hawaiian?" He must have noticed my confusion. "He *is* . . . . Don't let his haole looks fool you."

"You mean Hawaiian . . . as in blood?"

Sarcastically: "No. Sugar." Noa shook his head. I was embarrassed. "His grandfather—hey, you get some blood on your mouth—" I wiped it and sucked on the cut on my lip. "Anyway, his grandfather was pure Hawaiian. Well known. One of the first territorial judges. His great-grandfather, now get this, his great-grandfather was one of the Royalists who tried to put Queen Liliuokalani back on the throne. He was one of the young ones and he got thrown in jail . . . . Lemme clue you, Bud may not *look* Hawaiian, but . . . now what?"

Noa didn't finish his statement. Someone was yelling for him and he left in mid-sentence.

I wanted to be alone for a bit, to try to digest the sudden strangeness. I walked along the beach and around a rocky bend. Instead of solitude I found Kaeo, sitting alone on a rock, facing the inscrutable surf. When he saw me, he knew I knew. I sat on the same rock, my back to his side.

"Was my fricken fault . . . I wen' lay too much guilt shit on him, telling him he was too haole, li' dat.

"I didn't know he was part-Hawaiian."

"Ev'reday . . . Da t'ing is, no show, eh? I nevah know until I went his house one day and saw his mom. When you see her, you can tell." Then Kaeo snickered. "He got pissed off when I wen' ask 'om if he was adopted." I almost laughed, picturing Bud. We both fell silent for a minute.

"You know," Kaeo said, "just today he was telling me all kine t'ings about himself, about how he got into one classy school like Punahou on one at'letic scholahship, how he wen' fool plenny people by getting heavy into da academics . . . den he stahted hanging out wit only haoles—he could fit right in, eh? . . . said he figured da only way he was goin' get anywhere was by being full-on haole . . . an' dass true, right?" I nodded to affirm that I got his drift. "Da problem is, kinda hard fo' fo'get t'ings like eating guava and lilikoi off da tree, picking limu wit grampa, goin' net fishing, eating poi wit da fingah—" As Kaeo said this he gestured, dipping his finger into an imaginary bowl. "—an' all dat. Hard fo' get into all da competition shit."

"Yeah," I muttered, realizing at the same time that my right hand covered my forehead. Again we fell silent.

After some long minutes Kaeo said, "Eh. No tell nobody, but, ah, we wen' stumble across some . . . some bones."

"Bones?"

"Yeah," he said as I turned to face him. He looked distraught. I thought: *Oh, no. Don't you flip out, too.* "Human bones . . . had part of one skull . . . Buddy wen try pick 'om up . . . wen' sorta crumble in his hands . . . look like da bones was used fo' target practice . . . had lotta shells . . . an' I no mean *sea*shells . . ." Kaeo appeared to be fighting tears. He hid his emerald green irises by closing his eyes. Then he pressed his palms to his forehead. ". . . oh, fuck."

After our third silent spell, this time a brief one, Kaeo said with a sudden shift in mood and tone, "So, you writing all dis down o' what?"

"In my head."

He pointed an index finger to my chest. "Yo' heart, brah. Record it in yo' heart. Bettah dan *Memorex*. . . . Or bettah yet, in yo' *na'au*. In yo' gut, man." Then he got up and said he was heading back to the camp area to haul kiawe and help prepare the evening meal. When he was about thirty feet away he turned around and faced me. "One-fourt' Hawaiian," he said. "Dass plenny, you know."

I headed back slowly, feeling very much alone. At times I stopped and gazed at the distant slopes of Maui's seemingly twin mountains. "Flipped out" could mean anything. I wished Bud could climb up one of those mountains and pound out a message on large boulders, a message declaring his condition. And if I thought he could do it, I'd billy-goat up Kahoolawe's barren slopes to receive it. But I seemed to know better. Molokini loomed in the distance. Its name means "many ties," I recalled someone telling someone on the boat. Funny name for a cut off piece of volcanic moon, a perpetually crescent anomaly as "severed from—" as I was at that moment. No ties. Incommunicado. You walk around in a smooth groove for years and years, then one day you *turn and face the strange.*

Along the Hakioawa shoreline up ahead I saw a figure pulling something out of the water. A minute closer I realized it was a woman struggling to pull in what appeared to be a fishing net. I ran to help. The woman turned out to be Sue. Though I began pulling with her she seemed oblivious to my presence. I noticed she had some mean scratches on her arms. Her veins were popping out. The wraparound garment she wore was wet up to her waist.

"I'm not sleeping on the beach again," she said, finally acknowledging my presence after we had dragged the net ashore. "No way. This is our hammock."

Our hammock? By the way she smiled, easy-like, I didn't want to refuse. So this is how they get those makeshift hammocks, I figured. I had seen some of those comfortable looking things set up in the camp area. After we found a suitable spot, a clearing between five strong kiawe trees, I helped Sue set up the netting, lashing the edges, tying knot after knot to make our "bed" secure.

That night, after dinner and hours of conversation with whoever was around, conversations that centered on Bud or on me and my "planned article," I found my way to the hammock and climbed in.

Just as I was dozing off, I was shaken awake by Sue climbing on. "Hi," she said. "You sleeping?"

I groaned.

"Still worried about your friend?" I sat up a bit and shrugged my shoulders. "He'll be all right, you know."

"I hope so." Sue sat facing me in the darkness. She now wore loose-fitting jeans and a sweater. The lack of light gave her beauty an ethereal quality, and I suddenly wished I weren't so tired.

I'd have to describe the fishnet turned hammock. Not created for sleeping especially, it was wide as it was long; circular, in fact. And being lashed to five trees, it had a pentagonal, spider web-like quality. Big as it was, it worked only for one person. Once a second body was on it, every movement was felt by the other, making cooperation essential.

"I heard you guys last night . . . on the beach . . . laughing and coughing and —"

"You were awake?"

"Couldn't sleep. The wind blowing sand in my face . . . you guys making a racket."

"Sorry."

"Did you guys go walking in the bushes?" I nodded. "Spooky." Sue shifted to lay on her side, forcing me to shift too, and when I shifted by sitting up more, again she had to readjust. "So how's your writing going?"

"I've jotted down some . . . notes."

"You ought to go after a publisher."

"What? A publisher?" The sum total of my writing experience was a summer internship with the *Advertiser*.

"Yeah. Go for it. That's how you gotta do it. I've done some free —" she was jolted by my shift. "— some freelancing . . . and I don't even have a degree. You just have to write good, that's all." She seemed so spirited for one who hadn't had much sleep the night before. She could've had a conversation with herself. "How old are you?"

"Huh?" I was caught off guard. "Twenty-one. No, twenty-two, I think."

"You don't know?"

"Is it past midnight?"

She covered her mouth with her hand, then said, "Your birthday?" and at the same time jumped up excitedly, causing me to lose my balance. Somehow, she ended up in my arms. She kissed me on the cheek, whispering, "Birthday kiss." Then she said, somberly, "I'm twenty-five. Old, yeah?"

"You're anything but old. You're beautiful."

"You got a girlfriend?"

"Had one . . ." For some reason it struck us both as being funny. Either that or we had to laugh to ease the tension. "Do you have a boyfriend?"

"No . . . a husband." She smiled at me and I smiled back, but I was taken aback. She sensed it and moved slightly away from me. Silence followed. I had started thinking about Bud again when she whispered, "I'm separated."

"From what?"

"From *him*!" She looked at me incredulously. Her face wore a probing, slight smile.

"Sorry."

"No need." It seemed we both needed a bit of comforting. She shifted into my arms again, stared into my eyes, and gave me another birthday kiss, this one deep and long. This was followed by enough kisses for our next few birthdays.

"I love your eyes," I told her, as my mind swam in a happy, dreamlike state.

"I love yours." Sue placed her head on my chest. I shifted and let her head rest on my arm. In minutes she was asleep. Tired as I was, I lay awake for hours, reliving, reconstructing the day's events: the sleeplessness, Bud's crashing out, the long hike, the news of Bud "flipping out," the conversations with Noa and Kaeo . . . and Sue . . . and her crashing out . . . maybe that's how people change on Kahoolawe—in their sleep. *Invasion of the Body Snatchers* . . . the kiawe does look sort of pod-like in the darkness . . . God, I was so tired.

As morning approached and I lay still awake, I found myself stroking Sue's hair and face with my free arm. (The other one was hopelessly numb.) Her face looked impossibly tender in the zodiacal light. *Jesus. If she's been snatched, I want to be snatched, too.*

At daybreak the *Constellation* rocked gently in the waters a hundred yards offshore. Perhaps crew members brought with them news of Bud's condition.

I was among the first sitting on the shore awaiting our return trip to Maui. I sat next to "Uncle Leo," an elderly PKO member, a *kupuna* whom the largely youthful PKO membership sought out for advice. He chatted endlessly.

"Dey shoulda been here one hour ago. Already da tide coming up. Da surf getting rough. Stupid. Dey no listen. Wheah evrebody, anyway? Still sleeping, I bet . . . mo' bettah I take on da Navy by myself . . . . I wen' tell one of da EODs, when I was lighting his cigarette, I said 'Take one good look at dis face. One day you goin' be hunting me down on dis island . . . we friends now, now is a time fo' peace, now we bury da hatchet. Laytah on, we pick up da hatchet, dass Hawaiian style . . .'" Uncle Leo went on and on and I lost track of much of what he said. Then, when the *zodiac* was being steered in, he said, "Damn fools. Dey not watching da waves, dey not going wit da flow. Da damn boat goin' sink." Just then a large wave came and overturned the *zodiac* and its two man crew. Uncle Leo laughed. "Stupid . . . dey no learn."

The *zodiac*'s motor wouldn't start. Though we had dragged the inflatable boat ashore and wiped the motor dry, our attempts to render it useful were fruitless. We ended up forming a human chain in the ocean, passing the *ukanas,* the water jugs, and anything else we were handed as those of us in the deeper parts tread water for what seemed like hours. At one point the two EODs who had gone on the hike with us jumped in to join the human chain. Ohana style at its fullest expression, it seemed. Or, rather, *felt.* And this wasn't just something *Hawaiian.*

Bud would've got off on the whole scene. But I guess he had already created quite a scene of his own. He must've put Kaeo, Noa, and the others through a lot of shit. His "flipping out" was unreal to me, surreal, if you will. Like reading a newspaper. Like not being there.

I tried and tried to imagine the scene. Maybe to soak it for all the heart-bending drama it seemed to offer. But I wasn't there.

101

Still, I imagine it this way:

*Helicopter landing. Man on stretcher, or walking with
the help of others. Loud, whirring noise. FLAP-FLAP-FLAP-FLAP
. . . . Men in army fatigues jump out of helicopter and help carry
the victim in. Dirt flying, people sheltering their eyes from the
dust. An exchange of words, people yelling to be heard above the
din. Helicopter takes off. More dirt . . . and dust. Nothing but dirt
and dust, . . . dust swirling dirt in eyes, tears, squinting . . . and a
green cap flying around.*

That fucking vague. A fucking MASH episode.

I want to remember Bud for the brief — but intense —
moments we both shared . . . afterwards. 'Cause this is too fucking
vague.

I saw him only three times after . . .

The first time was him standing at the dock at Maalaea
Harbor. Bud had walked out of Maui Memorial Hospital without
a release just to see us return. He was all smiles, looking healthy
as ever, hugging everyone, helping us unload, downplaying his own
little episode.

And of course he was wearing his green cap.

It did seem that Sue disappeared fast that day when we
all returned — tired and browner. By the time we were unloading
she was gone. I didn't even know *how* she left, if someone had
picked her up, or what. She had squeezed my shoulders and kissed
me on the cheek as I lay awkwardly comfortable on the front deck
of the *Constellation* with the other tired ones and sea sicklies.
I did not open my eyes but I knew it was her. Nets of sunlight
warmed my skin. Her lips warmed my soul.

Before we left for our plane flight to Honolulu, Noa came
up to me. He came to say goodbye, and also to tell me (without
my asking) that Sue was going through some bad times, and though
she seemed to like me a lot, it would be better on all the hearts
involved if I kept some distance. I nodded, and before he could
leave I asked him if he sometimes thought that what the PKO was
trying to accomplish on Kahoolawe ever seemed futile to him, the
stuff for dreamers. "All the time," he said. "But if you can't dream,
forget it, yeah?"

Then there was the time Bud came to meet me many months
later, one cold, Manoa evening. I sat shivering on a bench outside

Hamilton Library on the UH campus, trying to warm up my insides with a cup of bad coffee. From afar, I heard — and others heard too, unless they were deaf — someone singing, out of tune and real loud, "BORN . . . in the USA, BORN . . . in the USA. . . ." A Bruce Springsteen song. Then, out of the darkness, Bud appeared, wearing headphones attached to a portable cassette player. A far cry from Kahoolawe, an experience I still struggled to convey on paper. Bud probably didn't realize how loud he was singing. Or didn't care. "I'm a COOL ROCKING DADDY in the US of A —."

And he was. Unhindered, unaffected, unassuming . . . *strange.* If America can produce guys like this, I thought, it can't be all bad.

Kaeo, Bud, and I — and countless others, I guess — always found ourselves wondering where being Hawaiian started and being American left off and how the two blended and why they mixed like water and oil sometimes. Kaeo continued to re-use term papers while trying to figure it out. Bud had moved to Maui, dropped out of school — Coach Tomey's dreams of a pro football career for him notwithstanding — to deal, perhaps, with his reorganized confusion, and had, in his own words, "just happened to be in Honolulu and thought I'd meet with the writer who can't seem to get over his writer's block and give him some scoops to get him going." By scoops he meant his looking into the Navy's plans to detonate unexploded ordnance at a safe place, the safe place being Molokini Atoll. Of course it meant destroying the coral reef and thousands of fish but who cares.

This was all serious business to Bud, yet he still expressed things in a way that made it clear that he hadn't lost his comic edge. In other words, he still was crazy.

The last time I sort of saw Bud was when his ashes were being scattered at sea. Not really scattered, rather dropped into the ocean off of Makena at sunset in a *pu'olo,* a ti-leaf container. It was beautiful. Sue and I returned the next morning at daybreak to find that each ash had become a sparkling light riding the crest of waves forever. We threw all the flowers we had gathered — plumeria, 'ilima, hibiscus, and others I don't know the names of — and red, orange, and yellow bougainvillea leaves . . .

Bud had been killed in an auto accident. Kaeo called to let me know. It was as if he had struck a hammer on a cracked boulder fifty miles away, and the sound tore through the sky in a straight line with the speed of a missile right into my chest. Then exploded.

Bud was on the losing end of a head-on collision. A car full of teenagers, driver reportedly drunk, had swerved onto the wrong side of the road on that lonesome highway between Kihei and Kahului. These joy riders, like Bud and I had been some eight months earlier, escaped serious injury. Bud did not.

Maybe Bud just wanted me to write. Or maybe he wanted to bring Sue and me together (I had confessed to him my lasting crush), I'll never know. But he surely succeeded.

Right now I am sitting on some pillows in a cabin on the slopes of Kula. This is where Bud lived his last days much like his first, as a Hawaiian. I'm typing on Bud's *Smith-Corona,* which is set on an upside-down cardboard box. Across the room, Sue leafs through his papers, laughing sometimes, sometimes smiling with tears in her eyes. I stop sometimes . . . to think . . . to rest, because my back aches and my head hurts. At times I pick up and again skim through the police report, which we got a copy of this morning. The same words always leap out: *Laceration of the heart. Death instantaneous.*

It has been quite a day. The funeral was two days ago. It was then that I saw Sue for the first time in months. It was a sad time to feel one's heart leap. It was then that I asked Bud's Hawaiian-looking mom if I could write a piece on her son. At that time I wasn't sure for whom, for what purpose . . . my head and heart weren't getting along. It seemed to be a gut instinct. His mom did not curse me or slap me across the face. She just stared into my eyes for one long moment. Then she handed me Bud's housekeys.

Today Sue and I tracked down Bud's car, not the Mazda *RX-7,* but rather the Toyota *Corolla* he had traded it in for. It had already been taken to a junk yard. *Everything* had been removed from it. There wasn't a cassette tape to be found. No rolled up match covers. No last words on a piece of paper. *Nothing.*

Then Sue and I searched out and found the scene of the accident. There we found skid marks, lots of tiny pieces of broken glass swept to the side of the road, burnt out flares, pieces of tire, thousands of cigarette butts, a Volkswagen hubcap, a flattened out *Gold Leaf* chicken box, a frisbee.

I still searched for something, anything, as Sue walked off in a sort of daze. Many minutes later, she found me, doubled over, clenching a green baseball cap in my hands. She caressed my shoulders from behind, letting her hair fall over my face. Then she whispered in a subdued sort of way, as if thinking out loud: "I see you found your bones."

After Sue had lifted me up and *medevac'd* me to the rent-a-car, she drove us back to Bud's place. When we were both feeling better we walked around outside in the chilly December air. It was twilight. We gazed up at the sky. The moon was three-quarters full. "Ever notice how the unseen blends with the sky?" I asked her.

"Oh, yeah. Always."

"That's his Hawaiian part."

I don't know if what I said was a trigger, but she turned to me and embraced me . . . real hard. It seems we both were a fraction of our usual selves, and became, in each other's arms, somehow whole. Afterwards, we walked back to the warm cabin.

And I began to write.

Between outpourings of words onto paper, Sue and I talked. A lot. She told me about her divorce, how she "zombied out" afterwards, took long walks, long hikes, cried a lot, tossed and turned in bed for countless sleepless nights, as if her bed were a cold, barren beach; how she thought a few times about me and how I was doing. I told her how I pretty much fucked up in school, never could get my papers done, and wasted a lot of time just thinking about such matters. I told her I often thought of nothing but her. We discussed her cultural confusion, my cultural confusion, and we vented our sanctimonious anger at the greed of men who overfuck *every*thing. Great way to start a romance. At best, like dancing on ashes.

If we did dance, though, it was a gentle rock, back and forth, to imaginary music on a 45 that some celestial deejay kept turning over and over. Joy . . . and sorrow. Joy . . . and sorrow . . . .

And, as if the world wasn't fucked, we made love.

105

The Vortex

Saint Paul in the Promised Land

We had to help him get to heaven.

Some would suggest that for Felipe "Paul" Magreal life on earth had been hell. But we knew otherwise. We knew that on a day-to-day basis he found private joy in the maintenance of his and other people's gardens, in playing cards, and in watching his prize Cuban fighting cocks when they hacked other gamecocks to death—though he cried when they lost. And we knew that when he still worked as a busboy he enjoyed the tips he got from tourists from places like Vancouver, Kansas City, Minneapolis, New York, L.A., especially those from L.A. "I hab one niece dere," he'd tell them in his Hawaii pidgin English-Ilocano accent, "in Los Angeles. He like me go dere. He like take care ob me." (By "he" he meant his niece, a nurse, a fifty-something-year-old woman who had a home in Anaheim. She often wrote to him, urging him to come live with her, promising to take care of him in his old age.)

Mostly, Paul enjoyed sitting around the TV with the other old Filipino men, some of them retirees like him, collecting social security or small pensions, though most still worked in some way in the daytime—cleaning other people's yards, driving other people around, clearing tables for tips, cleaning floors, cooking, washing dishes in hotels. . . . They'd converge around the TV in the living room they all shared, idly passing the time watching the likes of *Three's Company* reruns and *Wheel of Fortune* until something more interesting came on the tube—a boxing match, an old John Wayne movie, or CBS *Evening News,* for years tuning in to Cronkite, then later Dan Rather. The men would not sit passively then; they'd comment, sometimes to the point of heated

109

argument on each report, whether some skirmish in the Middle East, a flood in the midwest, some plane crash in Korea, an earthquake in Mexico. And when there'd be news about Hawaii, or the Philippines, or some incident in California—especially if it pertained to L.A.—they'd perk up even more, pulling their chairs closer to the tube, turning up the volume, whispering and shouting in response to events that struck closer.

Paul had lived in rooming houses during most of the thirty years that we had known him. We had first gotten to know him when our still-pretty-young parents moved into that small lane in Palama with four young kids in tow.

1957. Little Bobby enjoyed having dinner with the group of middle-aged and elderly Filipino men. They always had lots of rice and fish and soup that was green and tasted of boiled fish and watercress. Bobby used to sneak across the street so often in the early evening twilight that the men already had a bowl there ready for him.

Little Bobby had it down to an art. Though only five, he always followed the kitchen smell down the same intricate path out of our yard across the lane and through a hole in the *marungay* fence and up the stairs. In fact, he was stymied only once. One day, workmen had repaved the lane—a politician's promise, now that re-election time was close—and Bobby was hit and halted by the tar smell that had wiped out the aromatic soup smell, and he noticed that the road was too freshly paved for a barefoot kid to cross. One worker must have caught the sad look in his already droopy eyes and picked him up. Bobby pointed at his destination. The worker passed him to the worker beside him, who passed him on to the next, and so on, a bit of a circuitous pattern, but it got him there and through the fence and up the stairs he flew, heading toward the kitchen.

It was the community kitchen that functioned as the gathering place in those pre-TV days, for though television had arrived in Honolulu a few years earlier, it still hadn't found its way to their doorsteps. There they spent a thousand mealtimes, helping our skinny little brother fill out a bit in the process, talking boisterously, telling jokes Bobby could not understand and laughing when he pretended he did. One old man, Domingo, showed Bobby how he could remove his thumb and then put it back. Another one, Pedro, whom we found out later was a nephew of Paul's, could make coins appear from out of nowhere. Little Bobby liked the magic as much as he liked the food.

These same men spent their weekend days sitting in their spacious though dilapidated three-car covered garage. One day Bobby brought three-year-old Marlene there. For some reason that is still a mystery Bobby brought her right up to the meanest looking, gruffiest man there. It was Paul (Felipe in those days). Little Marlene looked up at the harsh face — the soupy, wet eyes, the high cheekbones, the chin whiskers. Then the face cracked a goofy smile. Marlene screamed and ran into the street and would have been hit by an oncoming car had it not been for the slowness to which the small winding lane stalled all moving vehicles. Bobby kept bringing her back, however, and because the men gave her candy, and the quarters and half dollars they pulled out from behind their ears, and made playing cards fly like birds then disappear, soon Marlene was having as good a time as Bobby was.

Mom and dad were oblivious to our hidden lives (all of us, for the older ones, twelve-year-old Eddie and thirteen-year-old Julie, had their mysteries too), as even the most conscientious of parents often are, just as we all were oblivious to the lonelier side to the lives of these old men as each retreated into his small room, confronting his own unique solitude, facing the evidence of shattered promises and token dreams.

That Christmas, Paul brought over two gifts, a train set for Bobby and a doll for Marlene. Dad made him stay for dinner. Later, Paul brought over some ribs from the Queen's Surf, the restaurant where he worked. Dad made him stay for dinner again. Pretty soon he was like family.

That's how we all got to ride in his '52 Ford, a spacious bomb with four doors. Paul began taking us to the beach on weekends, and when dad started working overtime a lot in his job as a painter and couldn't take mom along with whomever among us she could drag along to church on Sundays, Paul would fill in there too. He'd also take us to matinees, or for drives to the countryside, and he'd always buy us hamburgers and cokes after. Sometimes, he'd even taken mom and the rest of us shopping, helping to buy school clothes, toys sometimes, and because he knew of mom's penchant for saimin, he'd take us to out-of-the-way places where they made the best and we'd all wolf it down along with barbecue sticks and chocolate sodas.

Then we moved. We moved far away, to the Windward side. Still, that did little to impede our relationship with Paul (now really Paul, no longer Felipe, for dad had christened him with this Anglo-Saxon nom de plume for reasons only he understood. We never asked dad, "Why not the obvious 'Philip'?"). Paul, now driving a '55 Chevy, drove all the way there to pick us up, perhaps because he knew that we were now further away from everything, and that the added distance made the idea of going into town a more attractive proposition.

By this time we were well on our way to becoming a middle class family, thanks in part to the construction boom in the early sixties, and the growing strength of the union. Dad had started to make good money, so we got a mortgage on a nearby house, bought new furniture, and moved in with dreams of expansion. But it wasn't meant to be, for one day, in a strange industrial accident attributed to poorly set scaffolding, dad fell, and, lacking wings, plummeted to an immediate death.

Suddenly, we were back to being poor. We moved back to Palama, finding a place just two streets down from where we used to live, though not two streets away from Paul, for the rooming house had been knocked down and replaced by one of the many two-story apartments that began growing and multi-plying out of the concrete that had been poured throughout the area.

After a year in black and two more in mourning, mom tried working as a taxi dancer. We had no idea what that was, but it sounded neat to our youthful ears. The idea of it: our mother, a dancer. It sounded as neat as Paul's job sounded. *Busboy.* We didn't know what a busboy was, but we figured that if it's something you do at a classy restaurant in Waikiki, it has to be good.

It seems that mom's job led her to going out a few times on dates with men. She didn't seem too successful at that. Then she tried drinking. She wasn't to successful at that either, for it only caused her to wallow in the guilt she had been trying to repress. She blamed herself for everything that had gone wrong with our lives, even dad's tragedy, as if she had given him the fatal push.

112

Then she tried church, which she had given up while taxi dancing because she had to use Sundays to catch up with sleep. That worked, though she wasn't too successful at dragging us along. At first we were puzzled by her sudden change, her renewed interest in the promise of prayer. When we found out she was pregnant, it all made sense.

By now the older ones were getting married. First Julie, who in the throes of her burgeoning romance with money, married a haole M.D. who slapped her around a lot. (She got even with him a year later, in divorce court; there she put on a melodramatic spectacle that should have garnered her a best actress nomination at least.) Then Eddie married his already pregnant girlfriend, Pamela, like him a high school dropout, and so counting mom's there were two babies arriving.

Paul got a bit lost in all this shuffle. At first, after dad's untimely demise, he came around a lot, checking mainly on our mother, seeing that she was handling the loss okay, doing his awkward best to be comforting during her vulnerable moments. Plus, mom had to depend on him more and more for rides to the store and to church. But later on, mom began depending more on Julie and Pamela. They began taking turns taking mom around; they also helped with the finances and the supervision of us younger ones.

The babies arrived only weeks apart. The house was crowded for a while, too crowded. Finally, Eddie and Pamela took their girl-child and moved in with Pamela's parents in Waianae, way out in the Leeward Coast, and except for special occasions hardly ever negotiated the twenty mile trek to visit the rest of the family in Palama.

Rather than turning again to Paul for assistance, mama got a job as a waitress in a coffee shop, and began to grind out for us what became, all in all, a respectable upbringing. Us young ones finished high school, even went on to college, and though we still saw Paul on occasion—he'd stop by for this Christmas, that Thanksgiving, take us out for brunch at Easter—for the most part we went on with our surreptitious lives.

That is, except for our new baby brother Paulito. His given name was Jeremy but we all started calling him Paulito when we began to notice that he had that same crinkly smile that Paul had

and an obvious pull toward Filipino. Mom didn't like that nick-
name, but because of our persistence in using it, she slipped every
now and then—especially in anger—and called her son Paulito
too.

As if driven to the apartment house Paul now lived in by some
mystical force, carving a similar path through fences and bushes
the way his older brother Bobby had so many years before, Paulito
seemed to appear at the new, apartment style rooming house a lot.
Also, as the years sped by like the slot cars he loved to play with,
Paulito got into a lot of trouble. It started when he began cutting
kindergarten. Later, he'd set fire to things. Then he got into
stealing. By his early teens, he was using under-the-counter drugs
and was only giving mom a bad time. One day she yelled at him
without thinking:

"Why don't you go stay with Paul!"

"Bettah dan dis stupid place." She could've slapped him. Instead
she went to church and prayed.

So he did go to stay with Paul. For a time. We wouldn't see
him for weeks at a time; then, when he'd return, we'd kid him:

"Somattah? Tired of green gravy? Ready for brown?"

"What? Yo' chicken los' da fight?"

"Tired of living wit da bachelors?"

Finally, after enduring years of verbal abuse and numerous
moves, going from mom's to Paul's like a Duncan yoyo, he
retaliated by joining the U.S. Navy. Though only seventeen, he lied
about his age. By now Eddie and Pamela had four kids with one
more on the way, Julie had two more marriages, her third divorce
impending. Mom started to be known as grandma, her white hairs
confirming this new distinction.

When Paulito returned two years later, he went to a community college on the G.I. Bill. During this time he seemed to be
pissed off at everything, and wasn't afraid of letting everyone
know.

"Damned fucking world. Everywheah you go da same fucking
t'ing. Reagan. CIA. An' dey all running drugs . . ." He never talked
about what it was exactly that he had experienced abroad; he just
lashed out.

One day, Eddie, who was in town for the funeral of an uncle
who had died of stomach cancer, lashed out at him. "Hey, kid.

Whatevah's yo' problem, I no like hearing you swear in front of ma."

"Eh, she know da words."

"I no give a shit if she know da words o' not. Jes' no swear so much in front of her."

It was Paulito who notified us about the (other) forgotten man in the story of our lives. By now Bobby had been through his "exploring" phase and was somewhat settled with his girlfriend, Michelle, and Marlene had married a haole from the mainland, had moved to Colorado Springs, and was as busy making babies as Pamela had been.

"Paul stay in da hospital," he told Bobby one bright January day.

"What? What happened?"

"I dunno. I wen' to his house an' he no was dere. An' da adda guys no was aroun'. So I wen' ask da neighbahs. One guy said he saw one ambulance stop by da place, so I wen' start calling all da hospitals. . . . Found out he stay at Kuakini."

Bobby and Michelle thought they were the first to arrive at the hospital. It startled Bobby to see the emaciated figure lying on the hospital bed, gazing blankly heavenward, for Paul had loomed so large in his eyes and in his memory. Cancer of the stomach had done this to him.

Paul took no notice of the two visitors at first. Then his head turned, as if he sensed the presence of others in the small hospital room with the undefinable sick smell. When he saw Bobby his eyes seemed glad though there was no crinkly smile.

"Paulito jes' was here," the gaunt figure said. "An' now I see you polks. I tot I no see you polks again. . . ." Bobby couldn't respond. "How's mama?"

"Good. She doing good," Bobby finally said, his face tight, forcing the mask of composure on himself. "How about you?"

"Hoo-o-o boy, no can eat. Da stuff dey put on me . . ." He was talking about chemotherapy. ". . . make me sick. I try eat . . . I bomit . . ."

He paused. Then continued. "Boy, when de ambulance come I tot I been ma-ke already. I tot I neber see you polks again. I tot you folks porget me already."

"We wouldn't forget you, Paul." Michelle turned away.

"Now I happy. I see Paulito. I see you. Ip I die right now, I die happy."

A half hour later, in the equally foul-smelling corridor, Bobby took Michelle's arm and pulled her into the nearest fire exit. There he sat on the stairs and covered his face with his hands. His body convulsed. Michelle sat next to him, rubbing his back. After a few minutes, Bobby removed his wet hands and began to speak. "Man, dis guy did so much fo' us . . . fo' me . . . he bought me my first bike, you know . . . and used to give me bucks so I could go to football games, movies . . . I took da money like he was rich . . . but I knew he wasn't . . . man, he was always giving us stuff. An' what we gave him back? Shit."

"You folks gave him a family, Bobby."

"Give me a break."

"I'm serious. You folks gave him something he really lacked . . . a family."

"Big fucking deal."

"It is. To him it is."

So we all began to visit him. All except Julie, who was in the Orient and hard to reach initially, and Marlene, who was tied up with her family in Colorado Springs. We left telegrams for Julie and telephoned Marlene. Marlene, who had chosen Paul for her ninth grade "Hero" essay over the likes of Elvis, John Glenn, and Anne Frank, promised to fly in as soon as she could and made us promise to keep her posted. Eddie and Pamela started grinding out two long trips a week, sometimes bringing all five of their kids — not kids anymore, really, but young adults and teen-agers — in for Paul to see. Mama and Bobby and Michelle came about every other day. Paulito kept an almost daily vigil. Michelle started to feel close to the man she had hardly known, and we all tried to pinpoint the disgusting smell. "It smells like piss," Eddie said one day, but the rest of us argued that it had a more chemical quality. Though we never did come to any agreement, we all came to identify it with cancer.

It turned out that Paul had been taken to the hospital because of a bad case of bleeding ulcers. Then doctors found spots on his liver which they identified as cancerous. Then they found spots in the stomach area. Thus began Paul's relationship with anti-microbials and agents, with aniline dyes and arsenicals, with sulfonamides, and all those strange words we got out of the doctors, thinking maybe that's what we smell.

A month went by. Julie was back. Marlene and her family had made reservations and were on their way. Paul, though he was gaunt and still a bit weak looking, was diagnosed as being well enough to return to his rooming house. The doctors said that the chemotherapy had done its job for now. Still they cautioned us that the chances of recovery weren't too good, and sure enough, when Bobby and Paulito brought him back for tests, the doctors simply shook their heads. There were more spots. And since Paul was totally adamant about chemotherapy — "I no like dat kine . . . mo' bettah I ma-ke" — the only hope was the miracle of remission. *Remission.* We liked the sound of that word; it was as if one had completed some hellish adventure and now was able to begin another quest. Still it was a lot to hope for.

But it was far from over. We still had time to get him to heaven. After the new diagnosis, Bobby and Paulito returned Paul to the rooming house. Then Julie came over. Wearing a nice blue dress and heels, she started up the creaky, termite-ridden steps. Her heel bored through an area on a step where the wood was soft, and she had to slip her foot out and then yank her shoe loose. Then she slipped off her other shoe and tiptoed up the stairs in her nylons. Then, hit by the smell of cigar smoke, dust, and decay as she entered what she first thought was an anteroom, she fanned herself with her hand, realizing at the same time that the room served other purposes. She scanned the room, which was bare except for folding chairs and a TV set. Then she walked down the hallway and knocked on Paul's door. Bobby opened it. Paulito had stepped out to go to the store. Paul was asleep on a cot. Julie quickly scanned this room, looked for a second like she would faint, then turned and ran out in her stockinged feet, stumbling on the stairs, shoes and purse flying as she grabbed the railing. Bobby came running out behind her. He helped her up.

"Gee sistah, what you expected, *Dynasty?*"

"Shut up, Bobby, befo' I slap you one."

"Fo'get how it used to be already?"

"Jes' SHADDUP! SHUT YO' FRICKEN MOUT'!"

"No need worry . . . me and my friend Jeff gon' fix da stairs . . ."

"He cannot live in dis dump!"

Just then Bobby and Julie saw Paulito walking up the lane with an armful of groceries, eating an apple.

Julie went to her spacious but cozy apartment and made a few phone calls. Inside of an hour, she had set up Paul in Kuakini's classy care home for the elderly, *Hale Pulama Mau,* which had new everything and no sick smell. He was to stay there for a month. Then, assuming he'd be strong enough to travel by then, Julie made arrangements via long distance telephone with Paul's niece, the R.N., to send him to L.A., so she could take care of her uncle. Mom made her wonderful bean and oxtail soups for Paul on alternate days, the latter soup heavy with garlic, which she said was good for him and knew he loved. Again she visited with him regularly, as did the rest of the family, particularly Paulito, whose presence again was as constant as that of the afternoon shadows.

One day around this time, Michelle, while gazing through some family photographs with Bobby, trying to piece together the story of our family's relationship with the old Filipino man, said to her longtime, noncommittal boyfriend, "Gee, Paulito is there all the time. How come *he's* so attached? I mean, the rest of you have known him so much longer."

Bobby, who always seemed exasperated when anyone asked him anything that appeared even remotely innocuous, sighed, then replied:

"Two reasons. One, my little brother did live with the guy. I think I only told you that about fifteen hundred times. And two . . . well, he's sort of like Paulito's father."

"Sort of?"

"Well, the way I figure is . . . since nobody knows who his father is, and mom ain't talking . . . might as well be him."

"Could it be him?"

"Why ask me? Go ask mom."

When the month was almost up, and since Paul had gotten a lot of his former weight back and was cheery and looking just fine, Paulito and Bobby asked for and received permission to pick

118

up the old man and take him to the old rooming house with the new stairs and start packing his things for the trip to heaven. This time, as if seeing through the eyes of their older sister, the boys couldn't help but be disturbed at the condition of the place. They both felt guilty that they let someone they claimed to have cared for live in such cramped quarters amid the relentless incursion of dust, cobwebs, and mold.

The room was about twelve by fifteen feet, yet it contained the accumulation of almost fifty years: a small, raised cot with a stained, sagging mattress; shirts — mostly old silkie types that seemed to have been bought thirty years earlier, or bartered for more recently at the local Salvation Army store — and a few equally old-looking pants all hung up on a piece of cord that was strung across one side of the room; an old, blonde-stained chest of drawers that also served as a dresser, its top covered with an assortment of grooming paraphernalia — mirror, comb, pomade, shaving cream, razor — some papers, pencils and pens, and other dust-laden mementoes: faded photographs of Paul's family in the Philippines — parents, brothers, and sisters smiling against the squalid backdrop of a wooden shack with a corrugated iron rooftop; a photograph of a middle-aged woman — his niece, it turned out — standing in front of her tract home; a picture of Paulito in his Navy uniform; a night stand with a lamp and a bare bulb in the middle of the low ceiling completed the picture . . . except for one other item: the piece de resistance, a fifty-year-old, battered trunk that Paul pulled out from under the cot with Paulito's and Bobby's assistance.

The trunk told the whole story. It had survived the long, arduous journey to Paradise via Laoag (in Ilocos Norte, where the strong, youthful Felipe Magreal waved goodbye to his teary family, promising to make his fortune in that Promised Land called Hawaii and return and marry his beautiful sixteen-year-old fiance Elena, who waved through tears and smiles also); then the boat to Manila, where he encountered a boatload of Filipinos returning from Hawaii who told him and others not to go there, for, they warned, in Hawaii they would be worked to exhaustion just to earn their room and board (of course, Paul ignored them, perceiving shrewdly that they wanted to keep the secret of success to themselves, for he had seen some return in three-piece suits and Stetson hats, walking proudly through the barrio); then onto Yokohama where some Japanese joined them on board, seeking the same promises that Paul and his countrymen sought; then arriving at Honolulu Harbor in the spring of 1936. The trunk told the story of how he carried his then new trunk (a parting gift from his struggling farmer parents) through all this, and upon landing in Honolulu, onto the Waialua Sugar Plantation to receive his bango number, a warm meal that he'd learn he'd be charged for later, and a quick orientation on how long he and the other newcomers would work, when they'd get paid, and where they'd have to buy their goods—at the company store. Thus began the three years of siren to siren work, primarily of digging out furrows with hoes, and planting, with bare or gloved hands, the sugar stalks, weeding, harvesting. There was time for cockfights, sakura, and billiards for those who chose to gamble their weekends away, and there was time to be unfaithful to Elena (though little opportunity: there were few Filipina around, for Filipino men outnumbered the women at a ratio of about ten to one), but mostly, work took most of their time. The trunk also told the story of Paul's abrupt layoff three years later—he had been faithfully sending money home, scraping by on his dollar-a-day earnings, hedging his bets at the cockfights, hoping someday to make a killing and return home triumphant. The trunk told the story of how he nearly used it to clobber the luna who coldly announced the layoff to him with the words, "You're young yet; besides, you don't work hard anyway," the same luna who threatened the workers with a whip whenever they felt a bit feverish and had to slow down. The trunk also told the story of Paul's lost years before the big war, jobless, gambling and depending on other Filipinos to survive, saved only by the attack at Pearl Harbor, for numerous Japanese-Americans had to be replaced at their jobs, and Paul got a job driving taxi, driving American G.I.'s to the same Hotel Street areas he would later haunt, to the same dance halls he himself would haunt when the easy war was over, when he would face the tougher war within as he finally realized he had given up hope of ever returning to the Philippines and had learned to accept Hawaii as home. He searched the dance halls and other places, finding an occasional pretty Filipina face, but none was able to fill the void in his heart, the void created by the loss of, his betrayal to, Elena.

120

The trunk told the story of the 1950's, when Paul, seventeen years after arriving in the Promised Land, finally was able to pack his things in it and return to the town of Laoag. He had little to show except the deep need to see his aging parents, and a need, though his hopes in this area had long died, to see the beautiful Elena. What he found instead of the beautiful, slim sixteen-year-old he had left behind was a thirty-three-year-old fat woman (who looked ten years older than that) with four kids of her own in tow. Her husband had died, Paul found out, eight years earlier, during the waning years of the occupation of the Philippines by Japan, shortly before the arrival of General MacArthur. She had a son who seemed to be at least fifteen, perhaps sixteen. Paul dared not speculate as to who the father might be. He talked to Elena, who had recently remarried and was again pregnant, the way a stranger who has asked someone for a cigarette light would talk while striking the match, half-listening, wondering while chatting idly whether to pocket the matches or return them. And though Elena might have damned him to hell a million times, by now all was long forgotten, even the pain of remembering. And the trunk told the story of the monsoons that year, the wet trunk pulled out of the flooding room, the hasty trip out, this time by bus to Manila, and then by ship to Hawaii and into that rooming house in Palama. The trunk would be pulled out only three times more: the first time when Paul and the other old men moved out of the rooming house to make way for urban development; the second time was when Paul pulled the now clumsy and deteriorating trunk with his few belongings out of the apartment-type rooming house that burned down one crisp October night. Though newer and constructed more out of cement than wood, it burst aflame, and Paul (and perhaps the other men who lived there also) felt a private joy at being forced out of the urban lifestyle that cement had cultivated, for most of them quickly found another old rooming house where they could again build their chicken coops and raise fighting cocks and grow vegetables on every inch of available earth.

The one story that the trunk didn't tell was the story of how a young local boy entered Paul's life and consciousness, and then brought his little sister, and slowly made Paul a part of his family. The trunk didn't tell the story of how the father of the children christened him Paul, possibly because Philip (not to mention Felipe), the man felt, was too close to the derogatory "Flip." And the trunk did not tell of how, when the man died, Paul silently promised to help take care of his wife and children, even to the point of frequenting the dance halls when the wife became a taxi dancer, a woman who danced with men, mainly single Filipino men, to earn money to support herself and her children. Paul at first warded off his compadres, his countrymen, but in time realized it was not his place to. Though he had to take her home a couple of times, for the most part he watched and did not act, even when the woman drank too much and went off with one of the dashing younger men. Once he even danced with her; she didn't charge him; she was a little tipsy and told him to quit hiding in the corner and to join in all the fun. They danced beautifully . . . a rondella . . . but only that once, for that same night she got pissing drunk and threw up on the beautiful long-sleeve shirt of a customer, who slapped her. Paul jumped him, and, not knowing his own strength, knocked the fellow out and dragged the woman out of there. Down the creaky steps he pulled her, fast, too hurriedly, for again she commenced vomiting. She pulled away from him at the corner of Hotel and Maunakea Streets as puzzled young sailors in white stared in disbelief, she plopped herself down on the sidewalk, disgorged all that had risen from inside her into the gutter in the drizzling rain, and then she wept. And Paul, silent, behind her, wept too. Neither of them ever went back.

The third time the trunk was pulled out was when Paulito and Bobby waved Paul aside and together they struggled to pull the immensely heavy trunk from under the cot.

The trunk had survived two long trips to and from the Philippines, it had outlasted eight American presidents, three American wars and dozens of other skirmishes, it had survived the plantations, a flooded room and a fire.

And it showed.

The handle was now a piece of wire. There were scars from it being scorched. Water had permanently stained its leathery exterior. Rust seemed overstated all along the metal hinges and the steel-reinforced corners.

"Jes' need one new handle," Paul told Paulito and Bobby, who stared at the impressive bit of storage/travel material with a shared quiet awe. "Get one place by Gem. Maybe you can take me obah dere; maybe dey can pix 'om."

"Sure Paul," Bobby said.

"Why you no take him now?" Paulito stated. "I can stay heah. You can buy him some lunch . . . an' bring somet'ing back fo' me." Paulito handed Bobby a five; Bobby waved it off. To Bobby it seemed like his younger brother needed to be alone; he was holding in too much.

Bobby took Paul to Gem, a large department store. Near the entrance there were different shops—a snack place, a flower shop, a shoe and leather store. "Dis de place," Paul said.

Bobby and Paul walked into the shoe store. A man came to the counter. Bobby lifted the emptied-but-still-heavy trunk onto the countertop. "Whew," the man said.

"Can put one new handle on dis?" Paul said. "So mo' easy por carry?"

"Sure enough," the man said. "If that's what you want." The man lifted the large trunk to turn it on its side. "I could also replace these hinges. They don't look so good."

"How much gon' cost?" Bobby asked.

"Hmmmm. Hmmmm. Twenty-eight . . . with tax . . . let's see . . . twenty-nine, twelve." Paul looked at Bobby.

"No problem, Paul. I get 'om." Bobby looked at the man behind the counter. "How long gon' take?"

"I can have it ready for you by . . . Thursday."

"What's today?"

"Tuesday."

To Paul: "An' you leaving Friday, right?" Paul nodded. Bobby looked at the man. "Shoot. We come pick 'om up T'ursday."

As they walked out, Bobby, who was surprised that it was already Tuesday, took one look at the man who was now staring at the trunk and shaking his head.

Two days later, Bobby and Paulito brought Paul back, paid for the trunk with the spiffy handle, and took Paul back to the rooming house. Julie came by. This time as she walked up the newly-fixed stairs she seemed braced for the experience. And as she entered Paul's room she appeared to be in good spirits. Then she took one look at the trunk and went out to buy a set of Louis Vuitton luggage, a three piece suit, and a porkpie hat.

"Heaven has a dress code now," Bobby whispered to his younger brother. Paulito snickered but looked wistful, sad.

Julie then took Paul to lunch, to a Chinese place where she told Paul they made great abalone soup. She was to take him shopping after, in her Volvo. Bobby and Paulito hung out in the room for a few minutes. Then Bobby suggested they go for a drive and maybe pick up something to eat.

They decided to use Paul's '55 Chevy, which though it had a bit of rust was in excellent running condition. The two brothers, silently smoking cigarettes, cruised up the Pali Highway. "We should get pissing drunk tonight," Paulito muttered after a while.

"Nah brah, I t'ink I getting too old fo' dat kine stuff. Me an' Michelle—" Bobby took a drag from his cigarette, and didn't finish what he had started to say. So they were silent again. At one point, Bobby turned to look at his younger brother and in the silent way of communicating that he and his other siblings had developed in the closeness of their younger years said *OK, vent* . . . .

"You know, Bobby, da adda day, when you an' Paul wen' go Gem, I was checking out some a' da stuffs dat we wen' pull outa da trunk. Da t'ing dat got me mos' was dis papah . . ." He ashed his cigarette, then continued. "Right on dis pepah it says, in capital lettahs, ALIEN. Dey saying Paul one fucking alien. . . . . Dey have da fucking gall to call him one alien. He been heah fifty years, man, serving all da fucking tourists—"

"Paul likes tourists . . ."

"I no give a fuck if he love 'om o' hate 'om. *Dey* da fucking aliens. If he one alien what dat make *me,* bruddah Bob?" Bobby didn't respond. "What? You t'ink I dunno?" Bobby stopped the car, pulled to the roadside.

"What? Ma tole you somet'ing she nevah tell us?"

"Not any mo' dan you already know. . . . I used to bug her an' bug her. 'Who my faddah? I gotta know.' Den one day she stahted crying an' said, 'Dey came and dey went; I *really* don't know, Jeremy.' An' I said, 'Could it a' been Paul?' an' she wen' laugh. 'Anybody but him,' she said. 'Dass not his style.'

"So I figgah dis way: Ev'ry one a' dem is my faddah. . . . Ev'ry 'alien' is my faddah. Ev'ry guy . . ." Tears streamed down his face now. ". . . every 'buk-buk' dat washes adda people's dishes in Waikiki, cleans people's yards in Alewa Heights and up Nuuanu

124

. . . ev'ry 'manong' hanging out at Aala Pahk, Rivah Street, Mindanao Pool Hall . . . all da faces at all da chicken fights, dey all my faddah . . .

"An' Paul, 'cause he was so good to ma and da rest of us, an' 'cause he always give an' he no jes' take, he my true faddah . . . you unnastand?"

Bobby nodded, hard solid nods, as if his head were a hammer pounding a nail. Then he noticed the ashes that had fallen from Paulito's cigarette and onto his lap and started dusting it off. Then he said:

"Hey, I tell you what. We go get pissing drunk tonight."

The next day we were all at the airport. Everyone. Mom; Marlene, along with her husband and kids; Eddie and Pamela and their whole crew; Michelle; Julie and her new boyfriend; Paulito and Bobby, both feeling the painful stupor of hangover, both wearing dark glasses in the screaming late afternoon light. Even dad seemed to be there in spirit.

And, of course, there was the heaven-bound star of the day. Paul looked positively sharp in his three-piece suit, his porkpie hat, his one piece of carry-on luggage, and the maile-pikake and vanda and carnation and plumeria leis that were piled from his shoulders to his white-whiskered cheeks. And except for an occasional crinkly smile he betrayed no emotion. We all chatted idly, as always, relying on the older grandchildren to keep an eye on the younger ones who threatened to scatter at any given moment in a thousand directions. It seemed that only Paul—the grandkids called him "Uncle Paul"—was able to keep them under control, though he had to resort to the money and card tricks of old to pull it off.

Finally, the moment arrived. A voice coming out of the loud-speaker announced that it was flightboarding time. Paulito whispered to Bobby, "We jes' passing da buck, brah." Bobby, who was still trying to recover from the previous night's booze and news, the news being Paulito's drunken confession that he was positive that it was he who had caused the apartment house fire so many years ago, did not respond for a minute; then he said:

"Allstate."

"*Allstate?* Fucking Bobby, cannot get one straight ansah from you once in a while?"

"No. But actually, dass what I was t'inking. You know, you're in good hands wit' Allstate." Bobby sucked in a deep breath, and during that moment underwent an amazing dèjá vu. In the span of a second, perhaps triggered by the tarry smell coming from the airport runway, he was again that little child being carried across the small lane. Then the tarry smell became a soup smell, a green soup smell, the smell of happy brown faces. Then Bobby thought of the smell at the hospital. It smelled to him now, in retrospect, like a coverup. Not in the Watergate/CIA/Chile/Grenada sense, but more simple. It was one of those antiseptic smells used to cover up a more earthy smell, perhaps even the smell of death. It was one of those smells, designed not so much to enhance but to overcome other smells. Then Bobby smelled flowers, looked up and saw Paul looking straight at him, his face broken up with a smile, the exact smile Bobby had seen some thirty years earlier. He forced composure on himself, thinking, *good God.* "We jes' trying to put him in bettah hands," he continued to Paulito. "You know, like Dirty Harry, we gotta know our limitations." He threw his hands out, then, before Paulito could respond, he quickly added, "Oh. By da way, I fo'got to tell you. Michelle pregnant. We jes' found out." The others had just found out too, for Michelle, just moments earlier, had returned from a sudden run with hand over mouth to the bathroom and, upon returning to where all the women were gathered, trying both to keep a rein on the younger kids that the older ones had abandoned and converse with Paul, began to explain her "morning sickness." There were titters of delight all around and Paul was clearly tickled.

Still, for the most part, he betrayed no emotion. Perhaps, after fifty years in this sometimes hell, sometimes paradise, it was time to face a new Promised Land, still another promise of the good life. And as he walked away from us, the waning moments of sunlight ahead of him piercing our eyes, sending jolts of pain to the foreheads of the two brothers who had drunk too many toasts the night before, Paul turned to tip his porkpie hat, then, as if summoned posthaste by some higher authority, vanished to take flight toward the City of Angels.

The Speed of Darkness

Me and the Pacific have this thing, see?

And if you've never kissed wax while pressed against a surf-board like a lover . . . if you've never gulped salt water or gasped for air after being pummeled by a wave . . . or scraped your feet and knees on coral. . . . If you've never shrieked like a child with unconstrained delight while on a long, sweeping wave ride . . . or found yourself humbled by the perfection and stillness in motion of a tube. . . .

If you've probably never had to save someone from drowning . . .

"Drowning . . . drowning . . . save *yourself* from drowning," I began to say out loud as I downshifted then accelerated my Toyota Corolla hatchback onto the H-1 freeway on this hot August morning. "Money for Nothing" had just played for the thousand and third time this week, and as soon as I switched off the radio I found that my thoughts had again turned oceanward.

And it was oceanward that I was headed. That is, once I had picked up Doc at his home in Kaimuki. He and I were going boogie-boarding. We were going to ride big waves on bodyboards —not surfboards—made of polyethylene foam. I had just phoned him.

"The waves are calling," I said. He had taught me well.

"Funny," he replied. "I was just about to call you for the same reason. The south shore is up."

"Yeah. I know. And after having another fight with Diana—"

"You're not . . . *seeing* her?"

"No, no, no. Over the phone. Last night. She called 'cause she wanted me to watch Kai today. She said she has this seminar or something. I think she said at Kahala Mall. I told her yeah, sure, but I'd really need a dip in the ocean first."

"And wha'did she say? 'Don't hold your breath'?"

"Hah. Sounds like her. Actually, she said if I'd only stop trying to be another Ace Tiepel, you know, out catching waves every day, then maybe I'd get my thesis done."

"You just have to remind her, Nick, that you're out there *doing* research. The ocean *is* your topic. That's the trouble with women . . . they're even less reliable than waves."

When I arrived at his house, Doc waved from behind the screen door. "Hol' on," he yelled in garbled fashion, waving a toothbrush. "I'll be ou' in a min—" which actually meant ten.

Doc had been my instructor at the University of Hawaii's Manoa campus. The more he got bored with explaining the Doppler effect and Hooke's law to disinterested freshmen, the more his out-of-the-classroom passions zeroed in on Carl Jung's notion of the collective unconscious, and riding big waves. We had found common interest in the ocean, which for him was the Great Mother—with teeth; for me, nowadays at least, a place to sort things out. A couple years ago, I showed him a paper I had written for a General Psychology seminar, entitled: "Surfing: A Surface Trip or a Dive into the Mythic Center?" He said it blew him away and suggested I use it as a basis for a master's thesis, and together we came up with a proposal and title: "The Tao of Surfing: Physics and Metaphysics." Not knowing better, and silenced by the impressive babble that Doc spewed forth whenever he got off on the subject, I went for it. But I couldn't grab hold of that topic and just wing it; rather, I let it become something I retreated from whenever it presented its intimidating face. Still, Doc had been encouraging. In his interdisciplinary classes, where he got away with teaching a combination of science and mysticism, he always gave me A's.

And I'd give him rides, as I was doing right now, because his wife Elaine always took their car.

I opened the hatch door and Doc tossed his gear in. Now wearing cutoffs, a tank top, and rubber slippers (rather than the accoutrements of a scholar—pressed jeans, faded Aloha shirt, Birkenstock sandals), Doc was just another guy to hang out with.

We headed for Waikiki.

I had found it strange when he called me early one June morning a little more than two years ago and said, with no introduction, "It's six to eight!"

I was half asleep, and my muttered reply, after squinting to see the alarm clock, was "No-o-o. It's quarter to seven—"

"The waves," he interrupted. "The waves, Nick. They're breaking six to eight feet! They're calling out to us!"

By then I was awake enough to figure out what was going on. I immediately regretted showing him that paper. I regretted telling him I used to surf at Makapuu and Sandy's, because most of all, I regretted losing sleep. Yet I couldn't resist the offer. I remember waking my seven-months-pregnant wife with a kiss on the cheek, saying, "I don't know. I don't get calls from professors with such strange offers that often." I kissed her tummy and left.

It was a sun splashed summer, the summer of "Every Breath You Take," the summer of '83. I spent early mornings or late afternoons boogie-boarding with Doc—as I began to refer to him when he wasn't around—depending on our school and work schedules. Usually, I'd leave Diana waddling around the house, though sometimes she'd waddle and keep Elaine company—if she were coming too. We'd go to Makapuu, Point Panic, Diamond Head, wherever the waves were breaking. Most often we'd go to the Diamond Head end of Waikiki, a place called "Walls" (because that's what you slammed into if you didn't watch out), a convenient south shore spot.

One August morning Doc called and I told him I couldn't make it.

"Whad'ya mean," he said. "It's *up.*"

"I think I'm about to be a father." Diana's pains were five minutes apart.

"Boy," he said. "And I thought I had heard every excuse in the book."

Doc and Elaine sent flowers.

It's heartbreak hill to look back at all that. By the fall of '84— after the "Dancing in the Dark" summer—I had left Diana. Sort of. This was shortly after the swimming pool incident with Kaipo. And until this very moment, though I know why I left her,

I'm still uncertain as to why and how I let it all get so damned complicated.

And had I left my child, too?

Those days are colored innocent in retrospect.

Me and my kid have this thing: sea.

He will be raised on water. This I said to myself as I held him in my hands, Daddy hands, minutes after my wife's painful delivery. He had floated and kicked for months, Diana reminded me. And reminded me. A water baby. Before he learned to smile, react to our expressions, hug, turn over on his belly (to ride, of course), walk, say his first word ("beach"), before he showed the first signs of being a pain in the ass, I knew he'd love the water. When he swam inside Diana's round, perfectly-shaped belly, just by the way and the times she moaned, I knew he was taking practice laps.

We named him Kaipo. We discovered later that "Kai" is Hawaiian for sea, "Po" means night. Therefore "night sea."

Of course, we had no clue to its meaning when we named him. We just liked the way it sounded. And we liked the notion of giving a Hawaii-born, hurricane-induced child a Hawaiian name.

We were certain that he was conceived on November 23, 1982, the night that Hurricane Iwa unleashed its swirling winds and battered the Hawaiian Islands. We couldn't find Diana's diaphragm in the lust-inducing blackout that followed. And decided to chance it.

One stray spermatozoön, that nocturnal emissary, braved that night-sea journey during the blackout and arrived on Diana's fertile shores.

Thinking back, the name seems doubly right.

And we weren't the only ones. Nine months after *Iwa,* Hawaii experienced a mini baby-boom. Children with a strange calm in their eyes and names like *Iwa*lani and Nuu*iwa* abounded.

"It's the unconscious at work," Doc said, when I told him what I had learned about Kaipo's name. "Amazing. Conceived in total darkness. That's as magical a start as one gets. . . . And the kid's name conjures up all these feminine symbols. He's got all these things working for him . . ."

"Well . . . I just like the way it sounds."

The waves at Walls were bigger than expected.

"Ain't it great," Doc said, as we stood on the sand unharnessing our gear—fins, towels, gozas, Doc's clear acrylic hand board, boogie boards—Doc's an ion speed *Morey Mach* 7-7 with rail stiffeners and sleek design, mine a cheaper *Aussie* that bent a little in the surf.

While we wrapped the velcro'd ends of our board leashes to our wrists, I looked out and saw the rising monster. *Oh shit.*

I could never get used to waves bigger than, say, four or five. When you're in the water they loom much larger. Someone once told me that they—"they"; already it sounded suspicious— measure waves from the back, from trough to crest. With what? A metric? The scary thing is, when you're on top of one, looking down, it's over-the-waterfall time. And if you're thinking about the coral below the surface, about maybe getting hurt, then making what perhaps should be a once-in-a-lifetime occurrence an *every-day* one is a matter worth some hard thinking.

"Wow, the whole south shore is breaking," Doc said, disrupting my reverie.

"Yeah, it's heartbreaking." I thought of necks breaking, bones breaking. Paralysis. "I'll wait for you out here."

"Come on, you coward," he said, as he removed his wire-rimmed glasses and pushed his hair back of its receding line, "let's get in."

I don't know why I went with him on big-breaking days. I never did much. I chose to dive with my board under most of the waves. I got smashed when I couldn't avoid them. And when I got keyed up to ride the big one I'd always pull back when I saw the long way down.

But I did love it between sets. Especially the colors. Those lightly-etched blues of the sky, the range of ocean hues—turquoise green to turquoise blue in the shallow, marine blue to cobalt to indigo further out . . . and the white caps . . . and the copper and silver crests when the sun shone strong. And boy, when one smelled the salt air and felt the cool afterwave spray that tempered the heat of the sun, even the white-grey forest of hotels seemed almost tolerable. From a safe distance.

Mostly I loved it out there because it was the only time and place I really got to think. About my split with Diana, about Kaipo's fate, about Melanie, or "Lemony," as Kaipo renamed her, like little kids with untrained tongues are prone to do. Well, Kai was a few months older now and my relationship with Lemony (or "that witch," as Diana renamed her as-yet-unseen "replacement") a few months stronger. Though I had made up my mind to leave Diana before my strange encounter with this laughing girl on the beach, she blamed everything that went wrong with us on "the first girl you set your hungry eyes on."

"She has nothing to do with our problems, Diana."

"Oh yeah, sure. She just likes to date married men and break up families."

That always cut deep. "That's bullshit. We were already separated by the time I—"

"And I don't want her in my apartment!"

"Whadaya mean, *your* apartment? You've been long gone, Diana. Who do you think's struggling with the rent? I've used up my grad assistantship; I owe a mortgage in student loans. I can't keep borrowing. . . ." It was meant to be her apartment. I left her, but she moved out. And in with her parents.

"I just don't want her there, that's all." And she hung up. I felt a pain in the middle of my chest as I kissed my board in the gently rocking waves.

Although we seemed to do nothing but argue lately, I really felt for her. I had left her with a twelve-and-a-half-month-old to care for—when she wasn't teaching or grocery shopping or scrambling around for baby sitters—and she assumed a lot of what had been my responsibilities.

Well, maybe now she was beginning to appreciate my handling of the Daddy end of Kaipo care. After all, I did pick up after him; I wasn't that helpless. "Watch out, baby," I always would tell him whenever I'd catch him falling off a bed, a chair, a step, or over a stray toy, "one day the Daddy hands won't be there."

Now Diana did all of that while I spent a great deal of my time ocean drifting, mind drifting, replaying endless reels of our last months together, reanalyzing the reasons for the split. This was when I was not going through the strange ritual of starting something new with someone else, a ritual so consuming and precarious that one would hope never to have to do it more than once.

The swells had started to come in. They were bigger than I expected, all six-footers easy. I began to duck with my board under one wave after another, dodging wave riders and loose boards, waiting out the set by going under. When it was calm again, I saw Doc paddling over.

"This is great!" he said.

"Yeah, great," I said, with obvious mock enthusiasm. "Next time, let's go out when it's one to three." Doc looked at me like I was nuts.

"Wish I didn't have my damn meeting," he said, "'cause I'd like nothing better than to ride these suckers all day. . . . It would take a bunch of idiots to set up a committee meeting on a Saturday, on the last day of summer yet, when the waves are breaking."

Those words hit me. All summer long I'd been promising myself that I would ride the big one in. And here Doc and I were, on the last day in August, seeing the end of the summer of '85, another Spielberg summer, facing the rising prospect of another year in school—he the eternal teacher, I the eternal student—without a bang-up finish.

And with the challenge of another semester of thesis writing looming, and more matters of the heart to contend with, catching a gigantic wave seemed to be the only sensible thing to do.

"Here it comes," Doc yelled, suddenly, "my ride in." I paddled ferociously, like he did, kicked as hard as he did, but it was he who disappeared in the womb of the wave while I—after a gaze at the drop, and despite the adrenaline—pulled back.

Desperate to catch the wave that followed, I paddled hard and evenly, kicked hard with my fins, did everything right but take that crazy elevator down.

I got back to shore the hard way, by paddling in. I lumbered slowly through the sand, towards Doc. *Not good enough.* I kept turning to look back. I watched others ride with seeming ease. Kids were doing 360 degree turns with their bodyboards. Some even stood up, rode them like surfboards, risking the wipeout. *I want to go back in.* But I had to pick up Kaipo. And I wanted to be with the kid, too.

133

I felt especially bad because summer was over. Gone. The next few days before school started were committed to matters other than riding waves on little more than styrofoam. Besides worrying about Diana and Kaipo and Lemony and finding a job, what with loan payments, tuition, rent, all converging, I had to deal with the matter of my unfinished thesis. After two years of sporadic writing, the end was nowhere in sight. I had picked a topic as vast as the ocean, and it seemed to grow larger each time I drifted out to sea. Who was I kidding?

After Doc and I rinsed our boards, fins, and ourselves, I took one last look at the endless stream of gorgeous waves. *If you could have ridden just one of them . . . you just ain't good enough.*

"I don't know about you," Doc said, as we headed back to the car "but as soon as my meeting's over, maybe *before* it's over, I'm getting the car and coming back. Can't let those good waves go to waste. There's more to life than earning Brownie points for promotion."

"Well, I'd love to come back but I gotta deal with the little terror. And Lem—, ah, Melanie's expecting me to meet her. I don't know how I'm suppose to manage that, for one thing."

"Easy," Doc said. "First you pick up Kaipo, then you meet Melanie. Then you bring them out here and have Melanie watch the kid while you and I catch some waves."

"Well, I don't know if Melanie would like the idea. And if Diana ever found out that Melanie was watching *her* son on *her* island. . . ."

"Hmmph," Doc said. "Well . . . when I come back I'm gonna be here till nightfall . . . and even beyond that."

Me and my son . . . and Lemony.

"Beach!"

"What? Beach?" The little kid nodded and pointed to the orange boogie board in a corner of my apartment to make his point clear. We had just finished our noontime naps. I had been sleeping on my folding mattress while Kaipo had crashed out on my spare boogie board, which was covered with a thin slab of foam rubber and a sheet. Kaipo had gotten up before me; feeling his presence, I opened my eyes and saw the grinning face hovering

134

over me. At that moment I realized that I had been having that weird dream again, that ocean dream. I shook my head. "Kaipo, Mommy said 'No beach.' She said bumbye you catch cold." When I had gone to pick him up at Diana's parents' house, Diana had thrust him into my arms while warning me not to take him to the "b-e-a-c-h" because his nose had started to run. Till now I had noticed no signs of a runny nose.

"Beach," he said, nodding again, anticipating my approval.

"No. We go watch TV. *He-Man*. Or *Flintstone Kids*. Fred and Barney."

He shook his head. "No-no-no-no-NO!"

Oh, no. The little guy was losing it. The "terrible two's" aren't just something some psychologist made up.

"We go listen to 'mick.'" Kaipo's word for music. "Daddy play tape." I popped in a Police cassette. Sting and company were right up there with *Sesame Street* for Kaipo. I played a favorite tune of his and sang along with the chorus:

Roxanne . . . you don't have to put on the red light.

"Come on, sweetheart. Sing with Daddy. *Rox —*"

He started to cry. "NO-NO-NOOOOOOOOOO —"

"Okay, okay. We go beach then . . . sheesh."

Before we left the apartment I picked up the phone and called Lemony.

Rock-sand . . . . we sang in delirious unison in the car. Kaipo faked the parts he didn't know, and compensated by singing the parts he did know loud and strong. And way off key. We sang more high-pitched and giddily with each succeeding line: *ROCK-SAND* . . . .

Kaipo, restrained only by his kiddie chair, broke into spasms of laughter. It was a joyous moment for me. But that moment passed, and I saw this picture: a father and his son cruising down the boulevard; the son laughing purely, unconditionally; the father laughing too, but *his* joy suddenly darkened by all the reverberations his love for his son conjures . . . all the implications, the missteps, fears, the increasing messiness . . . all the elements that provided more context than a laugh should ever deserve.

But this was last year.

He stood on the shoreline at Ala Moana. Oblivious to refugees in string bikinis, high-thighed bathing suits, tights, trunks and cutoffs, oblivious to wild-eyed children splashing in the water, water that is opaque from tanning lotions, deaf to the screams of children on foam boards or in floaters, he . . . just . . . stood . . . there. Tossing fistfuls of sand. With his left hand. Then with his right. Then with both hands simultaneously. At twelve months, he had already created his own ghastly ritual with the sea.

Was he throwing fistfuls of existential angst at the ocean his father loves? Or was I overanalyzing. Thinking he knows. This one-year-old child-of-a-hurricane knows that *Daddy is leaving.* Then Kaipo turned around and threw a handful of sand at Daddy.

"No, Kaipo, no." I fell back from my sitting position on the sand. He giggled and threw more. I scooped up some sand and threw back, low, avoiding his face. *Sand fight.* He loved this game, which culminated with me rushing and grabbing him, then throwing him over my shoulder and running into the water. He shrieked with delight. I pulled him along the surface as he glided. A born body surfer.

Kaipo had no fear of the water. Ocean water, at least. I continued to glide him around until my arms and back ached. "I have to leave your mother, sweetheart," I whispered in his ear as I carried him out. "But I still need you."

No problem, Dad, his eyes seemed to say as he pawed my cheek with his fingers. *Just give me one more ride and it's cool.*

But that was last year. This all happened late last summer, a week or so after the incident in the swimming pool. It came to me as I watched Kaipo play, like most kids now, along the shoreline. He got sand all over himself, like always, but no longer did he rub his eyes with sand-covered fists when sand or salt water got in them. No. He was two years old now. Nowadays he rinsed off his hands in the salt water first. Then he rubbed his eyes.

He ran in and out of the shallow part, scooping up water with his green bucket, pouring it into a hole we had dug, then digging out more sand with his blue shovel. He lost his balance once, and fell in the water. In a second, the Daddy hands were right there, picking him up. Then I sat down again on the sand . . . and watched.

Kaipo wore his red-striped, green trunks, which had a string tie in front. Now two, his sun-lightened, brown hair curled out past his ears. And he had a killer of a smile. His mother's smile. A smile I only saw on his face now.

Funny thing, he had Lemony's color. A toast brown, somewhere between *Hilo Creme Crackers* and cinnamon.

And as I sat on the sand watching my son play, waiting for Lemony to arrive, again my mind drifted back to last year. Scene: Kaipo and Daddy meet Lemony. Setting: Same beach. Late afternoon.

She was the type that would attract attention—on the beach, anywhere. Her hair was a honey blonde, falling in waves over her shoulders; her eyes, though I couldn't tell from afar, a deep sea green. This was a sharp contrast to Diana's equally beautiful, long, black hair and small, brown eyes. With my mind set on leaving Diana already, and with no thought of getting involved with any woman, jaded as my hassles with Diana made me feel about romance, I wasn't about to hit on this woman.

Neither was I prepared to watch the slow but steady parade of men who would stop by her and try to start conversations. And I couldn't ignore her increasing discomfort as each guy made his calculated move.

This one guy just wouldn't quit. He even laid his towel down. By this time, I was playing near the shore with Kaipo, my back to the sea. Kaipo and I were building a sandcastle. Trying to, at least. At one point, I was watching the girl-on-the-beach scenario so intently that I didn't realize I was pouring sand on my son's head.

After washing Kaipo off, I continued to view the scene with increasing resentment of the man and sympathy for the woman's uneasiness. Finally, at some perhaps uncalled-for breaking point on my part I scooped up Kaipo and ambled on over to her. "Here, honey," I said, handing her the child, "watch baby for a couple minutes. I'm going for a short swim." The man, lying on his side by now, looked uncomfortable. I didn't see Lemony's reaction, I was already running into the water, refreshed and relieved, then suddenly worried that I had done the wrong thing, that I had left my baby in the arms of a total stranger.

But I was relieved to see, when I surfaced and gazed ashore, that the man was walking away, towel on his shoulder, and it looked as though Kaipo had made a new friend.

I approached them with apprehension, hoping I'd have the right things to say to her.

She spoke first. "Guess you mistook me for your wife." She smiled and licked her front teeth.

"I'm sorry, I—" I lifted up one hand, searching for words. She started to giggle. "I hope I, ah—" I folded my arms, lifting my shoulders. She covered her mouth, giggling some more. *Am I doing good? Am I doing bad? What?*

It was then that I looked down and saw that Kaipo had his arms folded, like mine, and he was leaning a bit forward, like I was, and, knowing him, he was probably mouthing what I was saying.

Lemony burst out laughing. I felt the crush of embarrassment.

Of course, this was Diana's cue. I saw her as she approached from the parking area. I'd recognize her ungraceful gait from a hundred yards. "My, ah . . . real wife," I mumbled. My words prompted a quick turnaround on Lemony's part. Then she looked at me with raised eyebrows and a smirk. *Sigh.* I grabbed Kaipo and took him to greet his mom. When Kaipo saw Diana he pried himself out of my arms and ran to her in short but quick steps. Diana pulled him up and hugged him. As she placed him down, she greeted me with an icy stare.

The sun had gone down by the time we started to walk away. Diana held Kaipo's hand. When I grabbed his free hand, Kaipo lifted his legs. A cantilevered bridge. Though we were being ground into reality as darkness settled in, Diana and I still provided the wings for our child's flights.

The Pacific and I, Nick . . . Christ.

Diana wasn't always like this.

Hawaii-born, natural charmer, Diana was one of those women for whom nurturing comes easy. She was fun to spend evenings with. We'd go to concerts, movies, watch TV. We'd study together at the library when school was in session. Sometimes, like when we had no money, we'd go for long walks on moonlit sand. We had gone to the same high school, Roosevelt High, in Upper

Makiki, but we never dated till college. Then I discovered that she wasn't much of a swimmer, and wouldn't dare catch a wave except in shallow water. And I slowly realized how smart she was. Schoolwise. All in all, she was an ideal companion, a nice way to face the post-adolescent world. And she did have a wonderful smile.

Then she sped through an apparently brilliant thesis and, while pregnant with the child of *Iwa,* received her master's degree in English, graduating with honors from the University of Hawaii. I, on the other hand, overwhelmed by the scope of my project, got stuck there.

Then Diana got her college teaching job, got her college teaching friends, and got us invited to different kinds of parties where we'd stand around with a glass of wine in hand . . . and *talk.*

Now for one who attended Roosevelt with the likes of Jared "Street" Babilona and star surfer Ace "Arc" Tiepel and other scruffy dudes for whom partying was hanging out in some parking lot with a Miller or Heineken in hand, blasting The Eagles, Zepellin, or Kalapana, if we felt mellow, on our car stereos, it was discomforting, to say the least, to stand around with a glass of wine and some chintzy hors d'oeuvres (like cracker and cheese) rather than generous pupu (chicken and sushi), trying to have decent conversations with strangers who'd inevitably ask:

"What do you do?"

Tired of explaining my thesis in American Studies for the umpteenth time, I began to tell people that I ride waves.

That always brought out interesting questions, like "Why?" And when I'd try to explain why and explain that I had a professor friend in the Physics Department who surfed with me and who one day had an experience not unlike that of Li Po, the Chinese poet, out at Makapuu when he, after being crushed by a wave, saw the moon and began swimming toward it and almost drowned because he didn't know that it was a reflection on the ocean's floor and that he was going down instead of up, I'd get the impression that people weren't really interested. Maybe I didn't tell it good enough, Diana. Or is it well enough?

Diana, on the other hand, really got into these gatherings. She got into these long conversations. About what, I don't know.

I mean, how much can you say about Emily Dickinson? Let alone The Great Vowel Shift. There she was, talking. And with that smile of hers, a smile that wanted *tenure*.

At one such party last August, at this beautiful, white, colonial style home in Kahala, I wanted no part of being sociable, so I escaped with my son to the swimming pool area. Diana and I had brought Kaipo along because Diana said she couldn't arrange for a sitter.

We had brought swimming gear: towels, bathing suits, changes of clothing. The invitation had stated: *Bring the kids. Come early for a swim.*

There were a few others in the small, bean-shaped pool. It was twilight. Music emanated from the living room. Some teacher type was plodding out jazz licks on the baby grand.

There were two boogie boards in the pool. One was being used by a father who used it to pull his toddler along. A mother splashed in the shallow part with her daughter. And there was an older child, a girl, swimming back and forth.

Then there was Kaipo and me. (Not *I*, right, Diana? *Me*, right? Right?) I carried him in my right arm above the water (we were in the shallow part) as I reached for the unclaimed boogie board with my left.

Accustomed as I am to the ocean, and not swimming pools, I didn't expect the sudden drop on the pool's floor and lost my balance. I tried to heft Kaipo onto the board as I fell but the board tipped over.

Down we went. I caught Kaipo in my hands and we went down, down, bubbles of water rising.

Oh God, we're falling.

Don't breathe, baby. Don't swallow water.

One day the Daddy hands won't be there. Those words, where'd they come from?

We go down . . . down . . . down. We hit bottom. I kick. Hard, seeing myself swimming to the pool's edge with Kaipo tucked safely under one arm. Agonizing seconds later, we rise, up, up, above the water. Kaipo gasps for air. I gasp too. But . . . can't hold him up.

We go down.

One day the Daddy hands won't be there. Excruciating seconds.

140

God, no. My baby. I'm dragging my baby down. Daddy hands . . .
don't wanna let go . . . pulling him down. Don't breathe, baby.
Hold your breath. No mommy air. Don't swallow water.

Help, God. Please.

At bottom, I kick. Harder. We rise, leviathan and child. Up.
Up, above the water. I see hands. *Hands. Mommy hands. Safe with*
Mommy.

I let go and went under.

I did not want to come up. I wanted to cling to my shame, let
it hurt me so good that I would never allow myself to go through
anything like that again. Ever.

When I did come up, moments later, when I could no longer
force myself not to breathe, though my breathing still seemed
more an infringement than a right, I heard Kaipo screaming. It
sounded beautiful. I approached my wife and son. "Sorry," I
muttered to her as I rubbed his bare back, his screams now sub-
siding to soft, steady whimpers. Then sobs. Those who had heard
or witnessed the commotion expressed concern. The hostess, a
woman named Jade, who wore a shiny green silk caftan, came up
to us and asked if everything was all right. She conveyed her
sympathy, then expressed relief that the child seemed fine. She
asked us what was his name. "Kaipo," Diana said, softly,
distantly.

Jade didn't get it, and apparently knew some Hawaiian. "Do
you know," she said, "that when it's pronounced 'Ka'ipo,' it
means 'cherished one,' or 'one who is cherished'?" Diana's eyes
rolled upward, then met mine for the first time since I had gotten
out of the pool.

"Yeah," she said, very flat and soft, "we know."

Later, when we left the party early, Diana's eyes bored right
through me. Those same eyes bored through me for weeks after-
ward. And no matter what I did or said in the weeks that
followed, her message to me was *Not good enough.* Finally, feeling
not good enough, I announced to Diana that I was leaving. "No.
I am," was her reply. She packed up, picked up the kid, saying,
"And don't you come around to see him," and left.

Me and my kid almost drowned in this pool, see?

" . . . and it happened so fast. I still can't believe—"

141

"Now you know what fatherhood is about," Doc said after I related the swimming pool incident to him.

"That I can handle. *Husband*hood, I can't. Not anymore." I told him how Diana had made me feel. I also told him about the woman I had met on the beach.

Doc, usually on my side, didn't try to be encouraging. "When I left my first wife, way before Elaine came along, I told myself, 'Who needs a swimming pool when there is the ocean?' Not that I almost drowned my kid in one."

"I didn't know you were divorced."

"Shit. Who wants to talk about that?" He took a deep breath. "The same things you tell me about this Melanie, I used to think about Elaine—this wonderful, crazy presence as undecipherable as the ocean. This Jade person, by the way, sounds like my *ex*-wife. . . . Then one foggy Christmas Eve, when Elaine had chosen to be with her folks and not me, I found myself—or rather, *caught* myself—saying: 'You're just as afraid of their freedom. . . .' You see, we men want the ocean . . . we want it all. . . . But sometimes a swimming pool, you know, in a certain kind of light, perhaps midnight blue, music coming out of the stereo, glass of wine in hand, can be pretty nice." Doc looked wistful for a moment, as if he were in another space and time, perhaps a better crossing of those coordinates. Then he smiled—tight-lipped—and nodded. "Pretty nice."

"So what you're saying is . . . the swimming pool is better?" Doc just shrugged his shoulders and lifted his eyebrows. No answer.

I was desperate for answers. And because Diana was keeping Kaipo from me—and Lemony wasn't quite in the picture yet— I was desperate from the loneliness.

I got so desperate one day I called my old high school buddy, Ace "Arc" Tiepel. I hadn't been in touch with him for a while. He had been the most popular guy in high school. He was already a champion surfer then. He wore his brown locks curly and sported a perpetually boyish grin.

Anyway, he married, of course, Sandra Franks, the most popular girl in school, and they had two soon-to-be-popular kids. I found out a couple of years ago that Sandra had left him and that they had gotten a divorce. I rang him up to see how he survived all that. To find out if there were wrist scars and other signs of divorce melodrama.

All Ace wanted to talk about was the surf. He still had this childlike passion to do the most crazy things. He talked about wanting to ride 40-foot waves the coming winter at Waimea. He said he'd ridden 25-footers a couple of times. I myself could not conceive of 40-foot waves. He said that when the waves crush you under you had better have great lung capacity. Or an oxygen tank, which he did use in experiments at Waimea the winter before. I didn't want to hear it.

He also talked about his daughter, who at seven was already a pretty good surfer.

"What about you, brah?" he finally asked. "Whatchu been up to?"

"Well, me and Diana are separated. We might get a divorce."

"Nah. Not you guys. . . . You guys? Boy, what dis world coming to?"

"I dunno, brah. How's divorce life anyway?"

"I dunno, brah." There was a pause. "I stay married again." A more dramatic pause followed this, then, simultaneously, we erupted in laughter. "You remembah Colleen?"

"Colleen?"

"Yeah, da chick that used to surf at Concessions. She an' me get one baby. Year old . . . an' one mo' coming. . . . By da way, I heard you an' Diana get one son, eh?"

"Oh . . . yeah." I got a clear, burning picture of Kaipo's face at that instant. I swallowed the pain. "He's a year old, too. Loves the water."

"Hey, neat yeah? Dey da same age. Ja'like us. Gee, what dey goin' be? Class of 2001. Whoa . . . space odysseys."

"Yeah. They're gonna do 360's on black monoliths."

"Yeah. An' den da surfboard goin' tumble troo space . . . at the speed of light."

"Nah. Speed of dark. . . ." And on and on. I realized I loved the guy. I had forgotten how Ace always loosened me up.

"Hey. You know what?" he finally asked. "We should make one faddah an' son surf meet. One 'Surf an' Smurf' meet, o' somet'ing."

"Yeah, we should." The funny thing was, he meant it. Ace made a living promoting surfing events. Sandra had wanted him to sell insurance, or cars, or VCRs. But all he wanted to sell was surfing. Surfing was his life. If he heard that someone was going to ride the biggest wave ever, he'd be out in the water, too. When he'd heard about guys doing 360's, that is, three hundred-sixty degree turns on boogie boards, he went out and did a 720.

Ace didn't answer my questions. But talking to him was comforting, a respite from the darkness closing in.

I was getting tired of waiting for Lemony—where was she, anyway?—so I grabbed Kaipo and threw him over my shoulder. He shrieked and dropped his shovel, knowing I was taking him into the water.

This time, however, he did something different. He didn't want to glide around—his usual favorite thing. It appeared that he had been watching other kids dunking themselves in the water. He wanted a part of that action.

And he tried. Boy, he really tried. He'd walk in until the water reached his neck, shriek, then grab me. Then he'd let go and do it again.

Then he tried throwing his head back. He'd let the back of his hair get wet, but he just couldn't stick his whole head in. Maybe the swimming pool fall did some real damage. Kaipo would close his eyes tight, though not his mouth, I don't know why. His expression was part grin, part grimace. It expressed fear, excitement, giddiness all at once.

Then a big wave hit me: There he was, at twenty-four-and-one-half months, already struggling to go over his own waterfalls. *Oh, my precious.* I hugged him tight.

I got him to glide after a while. He still could get into it, but only like how I could get into one footers once I had ridden a five. I took him out, rinsed and changed him, and sat with Kaipo on the beach waiting for that girl. *Where is she?*

During the time I contemplated leaving Diana, I kept on running into Lemony. She always hung out at Ala Moana Beach in the late afternoons. We got to know each other pretty well. When I did leave Diana, or rather, when Diana moved out,

Lemony was the first to know.

Then we began to take walks together, went swimming together, went to movies — a passion of hers — together. We did most of this when the sun was out because Lemony worked nights as a cocktail waitress. Sometimes we hung out in my apartment, sometimes hers. Her apartment was filled with intoxicating smells, cinnamon and ginger and herbs I didn't know the names of. And plants, wild ones. There were ferns everywhere. The music was wild, too. Lemony liked Brazilian/African polyrhythms and sambas. And reggae.

Together we shared delicious, wet moments, times when we couldn't get enough of each other. The problem, though, was this: the more perfect those moments were, the more guilty I felt about the woman who had to feed, bathe, and change the diapers of the child I had helped conceive.

And Lemony was also into boogie boarding. So now, I had another partner besides Doc. Work on my thesis ground to a halt.

Then this recurring dream I used to have years ago began . . . recurring. I used to have this dream where I was stuck in the middle of the ocean between Diana and my mother. Both would be in trouble. I could help only one. I had to choose. But I never did. Not in my dreams, at least.

I talked about this dream with Doc when I first got to know him. His terse reply was, "Now you have two mothers."

Now, Lemony had replaced my mother in the dream. Same situation. I had that dream again the other night. And again today when Kaipo and I were taking our noontime naps. Maybe I better ask Doc. It's just too weird. Right now, he was probably back out in the water catching waves.

Where the hell is Lemony? Damn girl has no concept of time. So fucking independent. Why can't she have Diana's punctuality?

Then there she was.

"Hiya babes," she said as she swung her backpack down onto my beach towel. She looked so beautiful in her green army shorts that matched her eyes and her coral cotton shirt that I immediately forgave her for her tardiness. "Where's Kaipo? Oh, there . . . ." Lemony snuck up to the little kid playing in the sand, said "Boo!" and Kaipo was suddenly a mess of giggles. She picked him up, held him at arm's length, and talked some baby talk to him.

145

He responded by reaching for her face and grabbing her cheeks, saying "Whoa—" Then she raspberried him (pthpthpthpth), he raspberried her back, then she raspberried his stomach and he chuckled. "I'm in love," she said melodically, hugging him. Visions of the wrath of Hurricane Diana notwithstanding, it was a wonderful sight to see.

"So," she said to me. "You wanna ride some . . ." she cleared her throat ". . . big waves?"

"Yeah." I had called her and asked her to come over with me to Walls so I could have one last shot at the waves of summer.

If Diana knew that Lemony was going to watch her son, while Daddy was out catching waves with Uncle Doc, she'd do a number on me that would make her other numbers—like keeping Kaipo away from me, like staring me to death—pale by comparison. But this was the only way I could try those waves again.

I carried Kaipo to the car. Lemony went to get her bike and we threw it in the trunk of the hatchback. Then I buckled in Kaipo, and off we ventured towards Waikiki.

"Tape," Kaipo said from the back seat and I directed Lemony to pop in a cassette. As we drove down Ala Moana Boulevard, we listened to the reggae sounds of UB 40. We passed the "Whaling Wall," a gigantic blue mural consisting of sea and sky and sea creatures, mostly whales, including one that soared upward way above the waterline. Kaipo pointed and said "Toto," for turtles were also depicted.

I shifted gears as we turned onto Kalakaua Avenue. While Lemony played with Kaipo, leading him in song, moving to the reggae beat, I drove in silence, mostly wondering how someone like Lemony related to the domestic scene she was suddenly cast in. Could she deal with less partying, staying home more, working toward building something with someone? Could she make a commitment? Make (uh-oh) sacrifices?

And could she want to? More immediately, could she deal with the fact that I'd made up my mind to finish my thesis no matter what, and spend more time with Kaipo and less time with her because there just isn't enough time to give, not anymore? Not when I have to adjust everything around her stupid work schedule. *Summer's over, ocean lady.* Diana knows that. Summer's been over for her for a long time now.

146

I looked at Lemony. Her innocent green eyes stared back. *Oh, no. I'll turn you into a swimming pool, too.*

I winked to hide my thoughts and she winked back.

I found a choice parking spot on the Kapiolani Park side of Kalakaua Avenue, close to Walls. Lemony and I unpacked our gear, unharnessed Kaipo, and the three of us headed toward the beach.

The waves were even bigger than they were in the morning. The biggest I'd seen on the south shore. So big they looked treacherous. The tropical storm in the South Pacific was really kicking up some action. It was choppy, too. The waves just kept coming in.

And, boy, was it crowded. All the kids who lacked good sense were spending their last days before school started getting smashed.

Lemony went in first. She had no fear of the big ones. I sat on a goza on the sand with Kaipo, feeding him. Diana had packed some food for him: a rice ball with ume inside, some scrambled egg, and slices of hot dog. The food sure looked good to me. I realized I hadn't eaten all day so I helped myself to some of Kaipo's Cheerio snacks.

"Watch, Kai, watch." I'd point out to him some wave-catcher doing something fancy, like standing on a bodyboard or doing a 360 and he'd point, too.

I couldn't even keep track of Lemony, so it was hopeless to try and look for Doc out there. I did think of Ace, though, when I saw his kid literally wrench his boogie board around, using the wave as impetus to ride *up* its crest, then down again. How could Ace not be here? I thought. Or at least somewhere along the south shore, because it's really happening today.

Lemony, to my surprise, didn't last long. "Too rough," she muttered as she dragged herself in. She showed me a nasty scratch on her knee that she had gotten from the coral.

"You all right?" I said.

"Yeah. But maybe I should stick to doing pool laps."

"Hmmph," I snickered. Was that what I wanted to hear?

I stood up too quick and felt dizzy momentarily. *Should've eaten lunch.* Then I gazed at the waves for one unembellished moment, put on my fins, grabbed my board, and left Lemony to

147

watch Kaipo as I went in.

It was rough, all right. It was a struggle just getting out there. Every time I dove under a wave, another wave was right behind it. I struggled against the current just to get nowhere. And then there were people riding right over me, forcing me to dive deeper, closer to coral. There was so much action—the churning, tumbling waves, the constant movement, frenzy and agitation all around. All the time. I felt alive.

When I finally got out beyond the crowded areas I looked for Doc. Couldn't find him. The summer sun burned furiously out there; it felt good to go under every now and then. When the sets came in I dove under each giant wave and during the brief moments when I could relax for a few seconds I watched in awe the crazies who were trying to handle the big ones. I saw kids flying through the air—vertical, horizontal, upside-down—on wipeouts. Sometimes I cringed. When a really big wave came in, after I dove deep, clutching my board tight, and then surfaced, I saw hundreds of body surfers and boogie boarders scattered like debris throughout the area.

I also saw some idiots on surfboards, which were not supposed to be ridden in that area. The thing is, when a fiberglass board cuts loose, it is a spear on the ocean's surface. And its skeg is a knife underneath. It pissed me off that the lifeguards didn't chase the surfers out.

One of the weirdest things I saw out there was this guy riding an almost nothing of a board, doing 360's and even double turns. What was he riding? I saw him flying through the air once and I think it was him I heard yelling with unqualified joy.

An even weirder thing I saw from out there was this black-haired woman who looked like Diana standing on the sand. I had been looking to see if I could spot Kaipo and Lemony. But I knew that this woman, who gazed seaward, couldn't be her. She was at her seminar at Kahala Mall.

Then I saw someone who looked like Doc talking to her. It must be my imagination, I figured. *That's what guilt and bad eyes can do. College ruins your eyes. Not just relationships. Too many books.*

I squinted, blinked, stared, and got crushed by a wave for not paying attention, but I couldn't see Lemony or Kaipo. She must have taken him for a walk.

I started blaming Doc for getting me out there when he himself hadn't shown up. I started blaming Diana for driving me out there with her correctness, her increasing intolerance of me, and her misunderstanding of my passions. I started blaming Lemony for being so innocent and for not washing over me completely and erasing all that haunted me. I blamed her for not showing up in my life seven years sooner. But then, Kaipo wouldn't have been. . . . I started blaming Doc again, this time for giving me concepts to apply to my woes, but no solid answers. *Give me answers, Doc. That's all I want. Answers. No more games!* I shouted to the professorial visage I had conjured up. *And I don't want the complications of my life forced into your tidy little mythic frames! It's all bullshit!*

I thought you wanted easy answers, Nick, the face replied.
No! That's not good enough! They don't work anymore!
Welcome to adulthood. The tight-lipped smile.

I dove under, leaving my board afloat, to rid myself of the taunting face, but the sickly green beneath was no relief. I came up and perceived, and not for the first time, the ocean's vastness, its all-encompassing flow. Ace knows how to ride with it, I thought. Why can't I do it?

Maybe only the ocean knows.

Maybe it isn't telling.

"Hey, Nicholas. What on earth are you up to?" I turned around and was startled to find myself face-to-face with Doc.

"I'm up to my ass in water, for one thing," I said quickly, regaining my composure.

"Yeah. Hot water, if you ask me." I didn't understand. "Could you please tell me why Melanie is out there on the beach with your son while Diana is less than a hundred yards away and she is looking for your ass?"

Oh, no. It *was* Diana. "Wha-wha'did she say?"

"She said she was driving back from a seminar at the Kahala Hilton—*Hilton*, not *Mall*, you idiot lamebrain, *Hilton* as in right down the street. . . ." He pointed, like I didn't know where it was. "Anyway, she was driving by and she saw your car. . . . So, then *I* arrive on the scene, having just passed Melanie and your

149

son, and Diana sees me, comes up to me and says 'I know he's out there' and I say 'No. He can't be out there. He's watching Kaipo.' Now you're making a liar out of me, Nick — which ain't so bad; actually it would help my reputation but . . . Jesus, for someone who's afraid of big waves — "

"Uh-oh . . . got any suggestions?"

"Yeah." Doc pointed south. "Tahiti is thataway."

I had to laugh, because I suddenly had this vision of Diana and Lemony pulling out each other's hair.

Then I remembered my dream. "Hey, dream expert — " I started to say. Before I could continue Doc and I had to duck under a gigantic wave. A set had begun to come in. A *big* set. "You know the dream I used to always have?" I began as Doc and I surfaced. "The one about being in the water between Diana and my mother?" Doc nodded with his board. "Well, I started having it again. Only now, I'm between Diana and Melanie."

"Good time to tell me," he said as we again had to duck under a monster of a wave. "It must be interesting," he added the second we surfaced.

"Yeah. It is. Today I dreamt it again . . . while taking a nap. . . . Anyway, in today's dream, rather than me trying to save either one, this time *I* went under. . . . Then both of them swam over to save *me*. And you know that Diana can't swim.

"So, anyway, Diana grabbed one of my hands, Melanie grabbed the other, and, at the same time, I realized that I could stand because we were in shallow water — "

"Look out!" Doc and I again went under to avoid the crunch of a massive wave.

During those moments underwater I again saw the dream scene. But it wasn't me holding hands with the two women. The wet, matted hair wasn't mine. It was Kaipo's. Diana and Lemony were dragging my son out of the water. Then Kaipo lifted his legs, again a cantilevered bridge. Without a Daddy hand to help. Or hinder.

I surfaced, hating myself, not wanting to continue my dream discourse. At first I didn't see Doc, then I felt his tap from behind.

"Never mind dreams, Nicky boy . . ." He indicated over his shoulder toward the shore. ". . . what's there is what — for the lack of a better term — we have come to know as *reality*. Now

150

whether you want a piece of that, and see that through, or hang on to your foolish, unfinished dreams, and blame your unfinished paper for all that is wrong with you, that is up to you. . . . But I'll tell you something," Doc continued as he now gazed out toward the horizon, "the biggest motherfucking wave I have ever seen is coming. And you're the only one in position. Go, you mother-fucker. GO!"

Doc's understated tone had cost me crucial seconds. I thought he was kidding until I glanced back and saw it. It was a sweeping, swirling hurricane of a wave. It was too late for me to go under.

So I go over. *Why not?*

Over the waterfall. "NO—NO—NOOOOOOOOO" It's spooky; exhilarating. The wave has caught me and there's no pulling back.

A surfboard comes tumbling by. *LOOK OUT!* I spin. *Ow!* Did it hit? *Ow.* Don't know. Not sure. I feel so alive . . . so numb.

Oh God! My leash! Cut in two. *Ha. Ha.* I hear myself laughing. *Ha. Ha.*

I regain my poise, move left, ahead of the break. *The flow, yeah, the flow. That ain't working, that's the way to do it.* People scatter. I'm running over them, *ha-ha.*

Ooh . . . dizziness . . . moving faster . . . faster . . . faster . . . too fast . . . *ooh, my head.* I must be having fun.

A guy to my left, spinning, moving right. Wonderful. Collision course . . . me and him. *Turn. Turn!* We both pull away. Start weaving. In and out. Just like that. He's good. Good as Ace. He is Ace. *Ace?* Ace. *IloveitIloveitIloveit.*

Faster. Faster. Yeah. board . . . almost lose board. Hold on. Ace standing up. *On what?* See no board. *IloveitIloveitIloveit.* I turn. 360. *Whynotwhynotwhynot?* "Whoaaaaa . . ." Lose board. I'm flying. Ace flying too . . . fast . . . too fast. I land hard— *ugh!*—on my back. This is too funny, too funny. *Ha-ha. Ha-ha.* I hear myself. *That's the way to do it . . . them guys ain't dumb . . .*

"Ace . . ." I reach for him, laughing, stumbling, falling, wave sucking me in.

"What you Nick, one crescent breakfast?" He too laughing. Our laughing merging. The same laugh. I drink salt water. Hear cough-ing, my coughing. See the Jack-In-The-Box tray I landed on. I look at Ace. Howls of laughter. We two, laughing, coughing, stumbling,

rolling laughing, waves tossing us. *Custom kitchen delivery* . . .
Ha-ha, echoing: *ha-ha, ha-ha.* "The flow, Ace," I say, hearing I
say it, hearing it echo, "the flow." *Ha-ha.* Stomach hurts. Too
much laughing. Echoing. Head hurts, hearing *Nicknicknicknicknick.*

I stand, blurt out headlines: "CHAMPION SURFER, ACE
TIEPEL DROWNS IN TWO INCHES OF WATER." He rolling
with my laughing, coughing with my falling, we both getting up.

Then I see Kaipo toddling toward us, his grin wide . . . face
wide. Lemony . . . behind him. I fall, falling, wave sucking me in,
spitting me out funny. I struggle out. See Diana. *Uh-oh.* Hearing,
uh-oh uh-oh uh-oh. I laugh with the hurt . . . the side of my
head . . . pain . . . dizzy. Hurricane Iwa again.

"Ace," I try to speak, "lemme lemme introduce—" He still rolling
over laughing. I see Kaipo fly . . . Lemony to Diana.

"Isn't your Daddy nuts?" Diana says. Kaipo pointing . . .
grinning. I . . . falling.

Diana sees Ace. She laughing. "The two of you again. Figures."
Doesn't suspect . . . Lemony. More laughter merging. Two boys
in washing machines. Laughter echoing.

Me . . . drowning in it.

Nobody's laughter was as peculiar as mine as the context
came spinning into view. Board spinning, bone spinning, wave
after wave after beautiful wave. I touched the side of my head, felt
the slippery wet lump and saw the expressions on the two
women's faces begin to change.

I thought I heard Doc's voice then. Or was it Ace's? "You
okay? You okay?" Somebody said Doc . . . Doc-tor.

Suddenly everything was swirling, a vortex of giddiness and
fear. I felt weak, as if a power line had been cut. I sought out the
calm in Kaipo's brown eyes. And I found it there, in the crescent
moons on the edges of his irises. Then his eyes too began to swirl,
a vortex as accessible as Diana's smile, Lemony's green sea. Perfect
tubes unfolding. I wanted to swim toward them and ride, ride
away from all the pain.

I never felt calmer; I must have smiled. Then, quick as light—
at least hurricane fast—darkness spoke as I blacked out.

Maka's Lei Day

April had left her wet streaks on the small picture window
of Maka and Pualani's apartment, and May, Maka thought as he
gazed out the window, loomed no different; still, after a month
of cruel, wind-blown rain, the window provided a clear, only mildly
disconcerting view of the cloud-covered Mount Tantalus, or, as
some Hawaiians still preferred to call this small but awesome
presence, *Pu'u 'Ohi'a.*

Maka dragged himself from the couch, and limped toward
the bathroom. He had been staring at the mountain as if it were
an obstacle he had to cross but couldn't quite get to crossing for
nearly an hour. He had crashed out on the couch again, slept
unbathed in his street clothes with the TV on, had dreamt bother-
some late-night-movie dreams, the kind where actors' lines penetrate one's dreamscape and are responded to; Maka, as he got up
to piss, was hit with that annoying revelation as he discovered
that his dreams, those visceral ruminations of memory and desire,
had been intruded upon by dialogue and other extraneous sounds
— not only sounds, but those light rays themselves, the magnetic
haze, that Maka observed withering off the screen as he flicked
the TV off. Then, after staring at the dark ceiling for what seemed
like hours, he crashed out again only to get up late — too late
for the job interview — and, in essence, the day, like a rain of
preceding others, was wasted. Worse, he had again failed to see his
wife, and their five-year-old daughter Lehua, off that morning,
and could only look forward to Pualani's disappointed face when
he told her he hadn't even tried for the job.

Already Maka had tested his wife's tolerance to its limits.
Jobless for over a month, he had grown increasingly lethargic.

153

To make up for this somewhat, he had assumed much of the household chores: the cleaning, the cooking, doing the laundry, handling the finances. But he had really blown it recently. A few weeks earlier he had been trying to balance his checkbook. Nothing jibed; numbers didn't match up. Beyond exasperation, he wrote out and mailed in the rent check, then headed out to seek a different kind of balance: the south shore was up. He grabbed his little used surfboard and headed out toward Ala Moana.

Maka parked at Magic Island, jumped with his board into the tragically beautiful deep blues, and fought current for what seemed like days. There was no balance to be found, no evening out. He discovered that he had lost something, something precious, for he wasn't as daring, nor could he last that long. And as he had for so many years, he found comfort only vicariously, seeing that out there, riding surging waves, another generation had staked its turf, declaring themselves stronger, more together . . .

Then, a few days later, when it seemed that matters couldn't get worse, the eviction notice came. Apparently, the rent check he had written out in hopes of some fiscal miracle on his behalf had bounced, bounced like a riderless, rudderless (for the skeg is removed) surfboard across indifferent waves. Maka stared at the letter, and the news hit him with awful revelation and proximity. Its tone was cold, indifferent. It had come from a management company. Not even a person.

That night Pualani, in a rage that seemed uncalled for, unless one were to consider that Maka's uselessness had been eating at her for weeks, threatened to leave him. That compounded the complication. What was it he had been fighting for if not his family?

"Family," Maka said disparagingly to the image in the bathroom mirror. Stripped naked now, he stepped into the shower and turned the water on as hot as he could bear.

Maka himself had come from a family of three. Though part-Hawaiian, and though he had been born on Oahu on March 3, 1950 (delivered by a midwife at his tutu's house in Palama while his father was in Korea, his mother often told him), he had been raised everywhere but — thanks to his military father. Maka had been raised in military bases throughout the world — Okinawa,

Thailand, the Philippines, North Carolina, before settling down somewhat in Orange County, California. For many years, all he knew of home were those military bases that took care to preserve the American way and make the world safe for tourism.

Maka's mother provided the Hawaiian part. She was three-fourths Hawaiian, and Maka's awareness of his Hawaiian heritage was gleaned from the photo albums she'd pull out of her closets every now and then, and more so the stories those photographs prompted her to tell with sometimes a wet sparkle in her eyes, stories of growing up in Kakaako, then Palama, listening to her older brothers and sisters singing slack-key tunes on the family's front porch on moonlit nights, stories of a poor but happy-go-lucky family that numbered it seemed in the hundreds when one accounted for all the uncles and aunties and in-laws and cousins, calabash ones too, and friends who gathered together on a regular basis to sing and party.

Maka's father, an Irish American, had a picture of the orphanage he had grown up in. This he kept deep in a desk drawer, and Maka would never have known about it if he hadn't been searching for some loose change one day.

What Maka remembered most keenly was when he came home from his junior high school one clear North Carolina day and saw his father's Oldsmobile in the open garage. He remembered thinking it was unusual for his father to be home that early, wondering, *Are we moving again?* He walked into the house and saw his parents sitting together on the sofa, his mother dabbing her eyes with Kleenex, his father holding her free hand. "Come here," his mom said to him, holding her arms out in what seemed to Maka an unusual display of affection. As she hugged him, his father, in his characteristically stoic tone, said, "You're gonna finally get to see your birthplace, kid."

The reason for the trip was to attend his tutu's funeral. The grandmother Maka had never known, couldn't remember having seen, had died in her sleep the night before. This was just three days after Maka's birthday, for which he had received, among other gifts, a card from her with a five-dollar bill and a note that stated, "When are you coming to see us?" and, from his parents, a 35mm Nikon that his dad had brought back from the Far East.

Hawaii came to life for Maka in the seven days he spent there. Using his brand new camera, and buying up rolls and rolls of film, first using tutu's five and his allowance money and later the five-dollar bills that aunties and uncles kept stuffing into his hands and pockets, he snapped everything up. From the air he took shots of the billowy clouds below, then the blue sky over the Pacific, then the seemingly tiny island of Oahu. Upon landing, he took shots of people's faces, endless shades of them. And later, he took endless shots of endless waves, shots of beaches wider than any he had ever seen in all the coastal areas he had lived in.

And there were some scenes the camera didn't capture, couldn't have captured. Upon landing, Maka and his parents were swamped with leis, and Maka was inundated with an explosion of things sensory: sweet flower smells, kisses on his face, hugs, laughter, as if there were no funeral to attend. And there were smiles, faces, wet faces too close to see clearly, wet petals on his shoulders, faces becoming more distinct, similar faces, unfolding like petals from the same bough, faces that were strangely familiar, faces that said, "Hi, cuz," or, "Aloha, Maka, I'm Auntie So-and-So, this is Uncle—"

Then there was the funeral. Aunties that looked so much like his mom wore the exact expressions of sorrow that he had some-times seen on her face, just as they had worn exact expressions of joy at the airport. There were hundreds of people there, most of them people he was related to . . . *connected to* . . . somehow.

And then there was the giddiness he felt when he put his camera down and leapt into the pond at Jackass Ginger, and the ecstatic tingle of leaping into the waves at Kalama, where his darkly tanned cousins, eager to share with the-kid-with-the-camera all their secret joy, took him again and again. Maka noticed with secret pride his own skin darkening and darkening, then he noted, with corresponding sadness, this same skin starting to peel off just when he and his parents were back at the airport. No camera could capture the private sadness Maka felt at leaving. His rela-tives had given so much of themselves. He was touched and he was sad. All he could conceive, from the point of view of a thirteen-year-old, was that he could not understand why he

156

couldn't stay, why the forced exile. . . .

He brought more than memories back, however. Now he had his own photographs to pull out of the closet. With pictures, he began to reconstruct his prior life, imagining how it could have been (should have been, he'd sometimes think) had his upbringing been a more Hawaiian one. He'd have been a surfer; he'd practically live outdoors; he'd talk the way people there talk, easy-like, with different rhythms and sounds rolling off his tongue.

This led to other fantasies, other lives. And by the time he and his parents moved to the California coast, his new-found passion for picture taking had become an obsession.

At night, alone in his room, he'd take out hundreds of photographs and slides that he kept stashed in his closet in low-cut cardboard boxes, and line them up, semiconsciously creating a chronology, a story. He'd sometimes sort them by color, or by the location and mood each evoked, dimly aware of some thematic significance. Sometimes he'd find dark surprise in the dreamlike effect created by seemingly incongruous, curious, accidental juxtapositions . . . all strung together. . . .

By the time graduation came and he had given his perfunctory flip of the finger to Franklin High in San Diego (mortarboard and gown left in the dust) he knew that he wanted to be a filmmaker.

Maka got out of the shower and gazed at the steam-covered mirror, feeling the heat, within him now, as the air cooled his skin. He put on boxer shorts, stepped out into the kitchenette, and reheated the coffee that Pualani had fixed earlier that morning.

In the fall of 1968, when Americans were beginning to realize that the war in Vietnam could not be won, Maka entered UCLA to study filmmaking. He was young enough then to be impressed by reputation, and UCLA's film school had a good one. Besides, it was situated near Hollywood, and Maka was young enough to be impressed by that too. He plunged right into the film program, studying set construction, lighting, color design; he took acting and art classes, attended hands-on workshops, went to on-site film shootings. Still he found time to surf at Malibu and to haunt the Troubador and the Roxy and some small clubs in East L.A. where he discovered people as warm as his relatives were, who took the loner in, who had similar pigmentations and concerns, and played wild music on their guitarons and tiples and accordians and vijuellas.

In the time it took for a reel change, Maka thought to put on a Los Lobos album. Instead he sat down on the couch, staring at the wall, sipping the hot cup of coffee.

But then there was Vietnam. It loomed over the university, violated Maka's conscience and consciousness with the daily death counts and on-the-spot scenarios conjured up on TV. It invaded campus life; political science classes overflowed. There was the matter of the draft, and Maka was young enough to be impressed by that too. Still, college — the one place where it seemed comfortable to talk and never worry about having to act on one's words — seemed a haven for Maka. Then he heard that two of his Hawaiian cousins had been drafted. And two more had volunteered. Awful revelation and proximity. Maka began to lose interest in the lure of Hollywood, for in his young, impressionable mind Vietnam held the greater attraction. He went back to basic photography, and began to shoot film exclusively in black and white. The campus rag published his photographs of campus rallies and anti-war demonstrations. Some of these photographs caught the attention of an *L.A. Times* editor. The *Times* bought and published some of his photos, then hired him as a staff photographer. One of his photographs, a close-up of a young female student's anguished face, lit by candlelight, backgrounded by the hazy glow of a thousand other faces and candlelights, was put on the newspaper's front page and garnered him a national award. Using this as leverage, Maka begged to be sent to Nam to "photograph the war." His boss said, "No, we got enough idiots running havoc there." Then fate intervened. The war, with its jungle rot and boredom, had lost its allure for a correspondent/ photo-journalist team, and they wanted out. Maka was teamed up with a young, black UCLA product named Walker Reed. Walker, who had had a reasonably comfortable middle class upbringing — both of his parents were teachers — had been covering Watts almost exclusively for the *Times*. He saw Vietnam as a break. "Niggers ain't de only ones getting killed dere," he said sardonically, in one of the twenty or so dialects he'd superimpose on his for effect.

"How do you know?" Maka replied.

"Actually," Walker added thoughtfully, "I don't know."

"Maybe we'll find out."

But first Maka had a little matter to resolve, and it had to do with his military father.

His father was in Thailand at the time. Though he had served his twenty and saw retirement as a welcome, newly paved road of opportunity (the road of the last twenty years too rutted, he'd say), the U.S. Navy had enticed him to slip into a cozy, temporary, post-retirement niche, to work as what, Maka knew not to ask. (A few months earlier, Maka had driven down to San Diego to spend Christmas with his folks. They had just moved out of the base and bought a house there when duty had summoned his father to serve its unquestionable ends for one last time. To mom's consternation, of course, for while her restless, rootless husband continued to seek answers to questions only he knew in exotic lands, as if there was something still out there to conquer (perhaps in the same way, at a much earlier time, that he, a dashing, young American sailor, had conquered the heart of a beautiful, young Hawaiian maiden (for she was beautiful then)), she would stay in that tract home alone, gazing at mementoes: photographs, jars of sand, black sand, from Kalapana, gourds, shell leis. As they sat at the table for Christmas dinner, Maka's father stated, "You have to wear your hair that long . . . and that stupid bandanna?" And Maka's immediate reply, thinking his father was putting him on, was, "Look at you. You can actually comb your hair now." Then he realized that his usually tolerant father wasn't kidding. It made for a festive holiday.) Now, facing his father in his unbelievably lofty setup, a mansion of sorts situated on the Thai beachfront, he heard his father complain of other things.

"They just kicked our asses at Long Cheng," he said, at first not even looking at Maka. Then he gazed at his son blankly, then his eyes narrowed. "This stupid war . . . it's sucking the lifeblood out of our country . . . it's killing us. Korea was bad enough . . . but this—"

"I'm going to Nam, dad."

"*Naw.*" His father grimaced as he said the word, as if he were

159

trying to articulate a gnaw, a stab of pain.

The scene was quite surreal to Maka; it appeared that he and his father had been given scripts to read, and were reading each other's parts.

"As a photographer . . . I want to do something worthwhile. I can't see people my age dying for—" Maka paused, searching for the words. "Maybe I can help capture . . . the wrongness—"

His father looked at him with incredulity. "Wrongness? How do you take a picture of a wrongness, tell me? Are you going to tell wrongness to smile?" He shook his head, blowing out air in exasperation. "This ain't the movies, you know."

"I know that. I—"

"Besides, you really think that a bunch of pictures are gonna make a damn bit of difference? You think there aren't enough pictures already? Let me tell you something, there's a lot of us in the military who want the war to end. We ain't *all* war-mongers, you know."

"I never said you were. I'm going, dad. I'm committed to—"

"Let me tell you something." He was suddenly very somber. "And believe me, this is based on a lot of first-hand experience. No matter why you go there, you'll get some fancypants notion of doing something heroic. You think you're there as a photographer, journalist, medic . . . but you're still there. Then when you see guys just like the ones you grew up with, their legs shot off, spewing their guts, you *can't* help but throw your fucking camera down and pick up a gun. It's too insidious, Woody. Weaponry's too advanced nowadays; war is too cold-blooded. Even if you survive, you lose your soul. . . ." While his father paused, Maka couldn't help but wish that he had had a camera on him all the time. He couldn't stop his wrist from turning, as if he were holding a zoom. He even visualized the movie. He was trying to think who could play his father. *Perhaps an older Paul Newman. Aah, but the eyes are too blue.* His father had sky blue eyes, not sea blue. He still wore his hair short, though, as Maka had noted at Christmastime, long enough to comb. Maka remembered the times when his father came home after long stints abroad. In his uniform he embodied for his young son the epitome of heroism. He didn't look like a hero now; still, Maka couldn't help feeling love for the man responsible for his brown irises

160

being speckled with blue.

"I'm getting outa this place, Woody," his father continued. He still called him Woody. "I'm retiring—for real this time. I thought I had commitments too. But that's all bullshit. Right now the only person I feel any commitment to is your mom . . . well, you too, but—" He blew out air, stared vacantly for a moment, whispered, "Vietnam," then shook his head. He looked at Maka. "Your mom doesn't need more worries. She's had enough already, putting up with me all these years. . . . I want to take her to Hawaii. That's where she belongs. I took her away from the most beautiful place on earth . . . and called it a career. Took you away too . . ."

"Join the Navy, see the world," Maka threw in, trying to lighten up the mood. His father wasn't listening.

"Your mom and I have been talking. We're going to move . . . to the Big Island . . . probably South Kona . . . get a piece of land . . . build our own . . ." Maka couldn't help but smile, and couldn't help but think, *This remains to be seen.*

"This is some hootch, dad. You sure you wanna leave it?"

"Just don't go to Vietnam, whatever you do. It's too damned high a price to pay just so people can live in stupid castles like this."

With those words he became aloof. As always. Forever the orphan.

Maka did go to Vietnam. His father was right. Two weeks into his assignment, a few miles south of the DMZ, he lost it. Amos Ledbetter, a part Kiowa, part Oglala Sioux who had acquired almost legendary status, had been shot. Maka dropped his cameras in the swampy muck, picked up Amos's M-16, and fired away at the unseen enemy like a crazed enlisted man. He fired and fired until something hot-spinning-pain-something-awful shot into his lower left thigh. He uttered a low scream, too ashamed to cry. A horribly low scream. Next thing he knew it was dust-off time, and his was one of the bodies being carried off into the chopper. At least his was a live one.

"Least you're being taken outa here a-live, photo-man," Walker said to Maka as he was carried off on a stretcher. Walker held the two ruined cameras. "Doan worry, man. I'll see that these get developed."

161

"Burn it! Burn the fucking film!" Maka caught himself saying it out loud, squeezing the coffee cup.

Two weeks in Nam. Struck down while still green. Maka felt nothing but anger; he returned home, ashamed to be alive and intact — except for one rotten piece of war memorabilia: a wound close enough to his knee to give him a permanent limp. He felt cheated; and worse, Amos didn't make it, and Maka knew that it was his fault. And then his boss at the *Times* wouldn't let him go back. In anger, he quit his job and moved to Hawaii, arriving on Oahu before the anger had a chance to subside.

Maka made his move to Hawaii in the spring of 1971; his parents arrived there that summer. Maka enrolled at the university at Manoa, to finish up his B.A., then work on a master's degree in something. Not wanting to seem overprotective of their twenty-one-year-old son, his parents moved not to the Kona coast as originally planned, but rather to the town of Haiku on the island of Maui, into an already built home, a cozy nook situated alongside a sloping street.

Maka met his future wife in a Communications class. After class, actually, when she caught him shooting pictures of her from afar with telephoto lens and confronted him with a grim expression that turned into a smile. Pualani was ethnically all over the place. Though she considered herself part-Hawaiian, she was purportedly also Chinese, Scottish, French, Italian, and Portuguese. There seemed to be many like this in Hawaii to Maka, where miscegenation didn't just seem possible, but inevitable. Pualani had strangely purplish eyes (Maka suspected the Italian part) and an easygoing style that made even strangers feel at home. She also loved to tease. When they first started dating, she insisted on calling Maka "Haywood," his given name, because she knew it irritated the hell out of him. "The only thing good about my name," he told her over margaritas one late afternoon, "is that it's two things that burn."

Rain stippled the picture window, creating corrugations not unlike that of a lenticular screen. The next decade and a half rolled by as if projected on it: *Opening scene* Maka walking alone through the university campus, Pualani suddenly materializing

162

at his side holding his hand as they walk through parks, *dissolve,* through beaches, *cut to* both of them standing in movie lines, *cut to* them lying in bed, *zoom in on* her face. *Fade out. Fade in to* Pualani's flower-filled graduation, *dissolve to* Maka's graduation, then a series of quick cuts: Maka at job interview at the local newspaper agency; Maka, along with cousin Kaeo, a newspaper features writer, and about two dozen others, heading out on a boat toward the island of Kahoolawe; Maka, with the features editor, who's telling him there isn't room for more than one photograph, "But they're great!"; Maka, again on a boat headed toward Kahoolawe, this time his dad included in the entourage. *Fade out. Fade in and zoom in on* Maka's mother's as she lies in a hospital bed, calm, half-smiling, Maka saying, "Well, do I have a brother or a sister?" His mom smiling, then sitting up to show him pictures of the tumor that had been taken out. *Fade out. Fade in to* Maka sitting at a table, working with an editing machine, *cut to* Maka facing a group of curious, curiously mixed students in his role as Communications teacher. *Fade out. Fade in to* Pualani slamming the door on Maka's face, *dissolve to* Maka and Pualani's wedding. *Long fade out. Fade in to* hospital-bright fluorescence shining on the face of the newborn Lehua, *zoom in on* her face as her mouth reaches for Puanani's swollen, partially exposed breast, *dolly back to* capture entire scene, with doctors, nurses, and Maka with videocam recording the event. *Fade out. Fade in to* Maka leaving the apartment, carrying some camera equipment, Pualani behind him, carrying Lehua, saying, "You can't sell that stuff, honey," Maka replying, "We need the money." Then, a series of quick cuts showing Maka at different desks, looking progressively bored, then walking away from a desk, then from a gray building, camera dollying back to show no one else around in the wide expanse of grass and low shrubbery. *Long fade out. Fade in to* apartment, where Maka is staring out the window. Pualani, from behind, asks, "Aren't you going to work?" Maka says, "I quit." Pualani says, "Why, Maka? At least tell me why." Silence. Pualani storms into bedroom, comes back out. "Just tell me why." "Lost my soul," Maka says in a voice that's barely audible. Pualani, exasperated, replies, "You got more than your damned soul to think about, you selfish sonofabitch. You got a daughter!" Silence. *Fade out.*

Maka limped toward the window, sucked in a deep breath,

as if he were trying to suck in the power of the now blurred view
of the mountain, then pulled the string that snapped back to lower
the blinds, heavy, like a theater curtain, shutting out both the
view and the rain of memories. "Enough, enough, enough," he
kept muttering. Then he saw the empty coffee cup in his hand, he
caught himself wanting to fling it at something. But at what?
He did not fling it. Instead he sat down, and as he had for
weeks now, he felt the tight grip of exile.

Then the phone rang. Maka stared at it. He stared at it
through four more rings, then he picked it up. It was Pualani.

"Oh, good, you're home." She sounded relieved.

"Why?" he said, reading into her tone. "What's up?"

"I forgot baby's lei! She needs it for the program today!",

"What program?"

"*What program?* Today's May Day, Maka. Are you that dense?"

Mayday? Mayday? Oh . . . May Day. Maka keenly remembered a
very crowded Brothers Cazimero concert at the shell a year ago.
One of the key coordinates in the map of island culture. A given.
"Oh, yeah, you told me the other night . . . May Day."

"Look, there isn't much time. Could you please get the lei to
her? It's in the icebox."

"Don't worry," he said, speaking faster. "I'll do it."

"Please hurry. The program is about to start. I'll feel so bad
if—"

"What time is it?" Maka yawned.

"It's 9:45! Don't tell me you just got up."

"No," Maka said, sounding angry, half-lying. "I've been up
for a while. Don't worry. I'll get it to her. I'll take it to her."

Maka limped on over to the refrigerator. His bad leg always
bothered him more in the morning, especially when he got up
after sitting or lying around for a while. He pulled out the
plumeria lei, scanned the fridge, then poured some Kellogg's Corn
Flakes into his coffee mug and added some milk and gulped it all
down. Then he went to the bedroom, put on his jeans and, after
a moment's hesitation, an aloha shirt and, still favoring his left
leg, dashed out of the apartment, realizing just as the door
slammed shut that he didn't have his keys.

There was no time to deal with getting the spare key from the
nosy resident manager. Maka popped out the kitchen window

screen, pried three of the jalousies loose, cutting a finger in the process, and dove into the apartment awkwardly, tearing his shirt on the metal louvre settings and banging his bad leg in a way that for a quick-cut second he relived the horrific moment when the shrapnel whizzed into his thigh, knocking him down.

Shhhhht-tk-tk-tk. Maka lay wounded. "Mayday! Mayday!" someone was screaming over the radio. "Delta Two . . . Delta Two . . . this is Bound Charley Six calling Bound Delta Two, over . . ." Pain; the sounds of moans, radio bleeps, and squawks; the comforting feel of oozing mud, then searing pain.

"Charley Six . . . position. We need your position . . . over."

Maka landed on the kitchen table, knocking down his coffee mug in the process and hearing it shatter on the floor. He saw the keys right there, next to where the cup was. He could have just reached his arm in. He grabbed the keys, managed to get himself upright, slid the jalousies back in, chipping bits of glass off the edges, then started out again, wincing from the pain that shot up from his thigh.

Holding the lei in one hand and using his other hand to partially shelter his head from the rain, Maka got into the beat up Datsun and started up the car. The engine made a tap-a-tap-a-tap starting sound. Pualani drove their better car, a later model Mazda, to get to her job on the windward side. Maka gunned the engine, lamenting its poor upkeep—he had even let the insurance lapse. It made a slight grinding sound. It needed oil; there was no time for that. When he eased his foot off the gas pedal it made a seemingly ominous cackling sound, then went back to its low idle tap-a-tap-a-tap. It sounded like a helicopter. It *was* a helicopter.

The helicopter picked up Walker and Maka and another writer-photographer team, this one representing *Newsweek*. At their briefing (or *de*briefing? Maka wasn't sure), he had heard military personnel muttering phrases like "media circus" and "helicopter chasers." He had quickly caught on that to most service personnel in Nam the media were scum, parasites, cataloguers of the freshly dead. He wasn't about to challenge their hypotheses.

As the car chugged on, the helicopter sounds got fainter. Then the car ran a bit smoother, and the helicopter sounds got louder again. Maka looked up and saw it flying over Punchbowl cemetery. This he had heard many times as he sped off to work in downtown. This time he thought not of Vietnam, but a movie based on that war: *Apocalypse Now!* In his mind he saw the opening scene, saw the ceiling fan become a helicopter blade. Nice trick, he thought. He had had no idea that Francis Coppola was just getting out of UCLA as he was getting in. He wondered if their paths might have crossed. Jim Morrison, of course, was the local legend there. He too had attended UCLA's film school. Then went on to mythical status with the Doors. Maka saw it all integrated in the film: Coppola, UCLA, Vietnam, the Doors, Jim Morrison singing "This is the end, my only friend, the end." The horror, the magical horror, he was thinking, the heart-rending proximity, of movies.

As he reached the underground parking lot of the Kalanimoku building, which housed the Department of Land and Natural Resources, Maka wondered how it was that he had gotten so far away from the world of film. Then he thought of Lehua. Everytime he pictured her face, everytime he heard in his mind the way she said "Daddy," he would feel that all the trouble, all the sacrifices were worth it. Lately though, once he'd drop her off on the days he took her to school, he'd sink in his car, and wish there were a better way. His job was drudgery. His title was Land Agent, a fancy name for an inventory clerk. He had been hired under some program that was meant to benefit Hawaiians, no matter how they think or where they came from, he thought self-deprecatingly. Then, because people liked him there—he was quiet, a family man, he did his work—they slid him into the civil service position that had opened up.

Up till then he had been taking advantage of all his sick leave, vacation leave, all the workshops provided for by his employers because he came with the label, "ethnically disadvantaged": "How to balance your budget," "How to do your taxes," how to how to how to . . . "How to find the job you're right for," "Improving your memory," "How to be impressive at your job interview," the latter a real joke to Maka, where two women with no sense of film technique videotaped him and others in a contrived job inter-

166

view to show them how poor their voices and postures were (or how nervous their gesticulations made them out to be). The real problem, Maka thought, is that with amateurs you don't get to do it over.

So, Maka said to himself as he watched the elevator light up on the number two, what's it gonna be like today? And then he wondered, *Is this the price you pay for getting married?*

Shhhhht-tk-tk-tk. The wedding had been wonderful. Maka got stinking drunk on Heineken and champagne. And when the band launched into the Motown medley that Kaeo had kept bugging them to play, Maka joined Kaeo on stage to sing backup. "We coulda been Pips, cuz," Kaeo told him later, when both were falling, laughing, drunk. *Cuz.* Maka liked that all his Hawaiian cousins called him that, though sometimes he wondered if they even remembered, even knew, his name.

Rather than becoming Pips, Maka and Kaeo later went to Kahoolawe, at Kaeo's urging. Kaeo reminded him over and over that some people have a hard time taking what they see there. "Don't worry, I've seen the Badlands." Maka began to get the idea that Kaeo was trying to prepare him for something traumatic.

It's beautiful, Maka thought when they first landed. The charcoal-grey sand sparkled even in daylight, and the island seemed completely unembellished by the trappings of civilization. And the trees were . . . just wild. But that was the shoreline of Hakioawa. A mile west, along the rugged coast, was Shipwreck's Cove, a debris laden area filled with everything from smoothed glass and tennis balls to beer cans and plastic jars and driftwood. And the further inland Maka hiked, the more he thought of himself as a Marlow (or a Captain Willard) being led into the heart of some undecipherable darkness. But it wasn't Conrad or Coppola, or Africa or Vietnam that his mind was driven to as the branch of a kiawe that Kaeo had bent forward flung back and stung his cheek, but the Badlands.

The Black Hills, Summer, 1968. Maka and his "Indian guide," actually his best friend, Jimmy Two Feathers, (who'd claim sometimes that it was actually "Two Fathers," that his parentage

167

was suspect; then he'd laugh and the listener would realize he'd been put-on), a full-blooded Oglala Sioux, had just been to the tourist trap of Mount Rushmore. Maka had taken a lot of pictures, more out of habit than anything else. Having just graduated, Maka and Jimmy were on a cross country tour in a broken down Ford pickup that Jimmy's father, a Navy man, like Maka's father had been, had bequeathed to him as a graduation present. They were "playing it by ear," sometimes just going with the flow of rock 'n' roll on the radio. "Wanna check out the Badlands?" Jimmy said, as they sat in the kerosene-lit, starlit night, hunkering over a fire they had built using mesquite as firewood, having run out of sterno two nights earlier.

"Sure. Whatever you say, as long as there's air-conditioning." It was hot, even at night.

The next day they drove along Highway 46. When they first sighted the Badlands from a lookout point, Maka was stunned.

"Here you go, Indian Country," Jimmy said. "Wanna ride through?"

Maka didn't answer. He stared at the eerie rock formations, said to have been caused by erosion. To him it seemed like devil country, like how the world would look after a hellish fire raged through and destroyed everything that lived. No one lived there (save Satan, perhaps); nothing grew there.

"Nobody live heah." Maka suddenly heard Kaeo's voice. "Not any moah, unless you considah da Navy guys stationed at Haki-oawa. "An' because a' da erosion an' da bombing, hahdly anyt'ing grow heah."

Kahoolawe. Known to ancient Hawaiians as "Kohe Malama-lama o Kanaloa." Missionaries were appalled by the term "Kohe," which meant "vagina," failing to appreciate the implications of the total phrase, the nurturing and enlightenment it suggested.

And so the name change, like so many other name changes. Like Tantalus for *'Ohi'a. What's the Indian name for Mount Rushmore?* Maka wondered. And what about his name changes? *You strip it of its true name, at least the one that suggests more accurately its purpose, its function, its essence, then you can send the U.S. Navy over to bomb the hell out of it.* Or into it. Phallic missiles sailing into wasted, indifferent vaginas.

168

Names. Names. Indian Jimmy (of course to Columbus they all were Indians; whether the *Nina*, the *Pinta*, and the *Santa Maria* had sailed into Bombay, bumped into "America" as they did, or showed up on the populated shores of Hakioawa, he would have declared the people "Indians," in the name of Spain, and then proceed to make further changes), Indian Jimmy could joke about those Anglo-Saxonized Indian names, including his own. He'd even make up some; he'd call himself "Running Scared Shitless," or mutter a pseudo-Sioux incantation, the kind he picked up more from movies than ancestors, and translate it: "He-Who-Dances-A-Mean-Fox-Trot." And while they watched the roaring fire send out its smoke and cinders toward the warm deep blue blanket of August sky, he added a new one: "I coulda been 'Jimmy Rising Up Sideways,' since I used to have a passion for escalators."

Jimmy, the class clown at Roosevelt Franklin High, had written in the school yearbook (below a drawing of himself wearing sunglasses and a headband with two feathers) that his goal in life was to be one helluva drunk Indian who lived in a teepee. Maka himself had written, under his self-shot class photograph, under the name Haywood Makena Davis, the middle name a misprint of Makani (which he didn't mind at the time, for rather than conjuring up some gentle wind it conjured up the place on Maui where his parents had spent their honeymoon, as verified by his mother's photographs of the place), "Born to Surf." By the time the yearbook came out, he was embarrassed by the attitude that it conjured in his mind, and had been so ever since.

Maka had thought that the Badlands would make a great backdrop for a photograph of his friend, since after the summer they were going to part ways. When Jimmy saw the camera aimed at him he suddenly looked real grim, blocked his hands with his face, and said, "No pictures, please."

"What. Your name's 'Jimmy No Pictures, Please' now?"

"Come on," he said, pushing Maka's camera away from his face. "I'm not kidding." Maka found out later that Jimmy, like the famous Oglala Sioux Crazy Horse, had some crazy Indian notion that to take one's picture would cost that someone his shadow and consequently shorten his life. Maka didn't know that at the time. But he knew enough even then to say:

"What's a photograph but a better drawing?"

169

"Ah, sorry, cuz, but dey no like you take pikchahs." This was Maka's second time on Kahoolawe. This time his father had come along too. This was November, the opening of the Makahiki season. People there were dressed for ceremony, the women in pa'us, the men in malos. "You see, cuz, dey goin' do one religious ceremony, an' kinda sacred, aah? Dey worried about da *mana.*" Maka had already put the camera away. By this time he wondered why he bothered taking pictures.

It seemed that his father made the adjustment to Kahoolawe better than he did. Perhaps out of guilt Retired Captain James L. Davis did quite a turnaround, and openly denounced the Navy for its use of the island for target practice. He had gone back to Maui with an altered view of American culture's superimposition on Hawaiian culture. He was to return to Kahoolawe many times more. "When one appropriates land and culture," he wrote to Maka one day in one of his more lucid moments in an otherwise long, rambling letter, "one can decide what is appropriate."

No sooner had Maka arrived at work than he found himself back in the elevator, camera in hand, riding down to the basement with a couple of his fellow workers from Land Management. In the parking lot he saw a lot of Land Cruisers, jeeps. *What section are these guys from?*

"You know how to take pictures?" his supervisor had asked moments earlier. He had nodded quickly. Anything to relieve the boredom. "Good," the supe said as he handed Maka a Polaroid.

He was twenty-two, going on fifty. He was the same age that most of the LT's seemed to be. The grunts all looked eighteen to Maka and Walker—pimple-faced kids right out of high school.

Maka *did* want to capture the faces of war.

He got into a jeep.

He did not know where they were going. All he knew was he would get to escape the boredom of checking reams and reams of IBM printouts, a task in which he buried himself day after day to assess what piece of state land was being used by whom and for what (a hopeless task, for Maka had calculated that eons from now, when he was very grey above the ears and had finally gotten through the pile, all the data would have been outdated and some guy with a dolly would be delivering a new pile for him to start over again).

It turned out they were headed east, in the Hawaii Kai direction.

Maka drove toward Kaiulani Elementary School (near Pualani's tutukane's house; he picked Lehua up after school), the lei on the front passenger seat. He hated the old Datsun, not because of the rust and torn up seats, not because the oil leaked and the car died off a lot, not because of the crying need it had for shock absorption, and not because of the lack of music due to a radio that had just chosen to quit recently, but rather because the car was a standard transmission and it murdered his leg to have to work the clutch.

As Maka got onto the H-1 headed west, he found himself on the H-1 moving east.

Where are we going? he wondered, as he gazed down at the sorry piece of photo equipment on his lap. This is Hawaii, not Vietnam.

Actually there was nothing at all Vietnamese about it, and yet . . . there was. Maka could smell it. He could smell it in the jeeps, in the raid-like atmosphere; more so, in the attitudes of the men. Yes, he smelled it in their attitudes.

Maka heard a grinding sound. His first thought was to feel sorry for the unlucky motherfucker whose car had churned out that awful noise. His second thought wasn't even a thought; rather it was a dim but immediate revelation of awful juxtaposition and proximity that it was the Datsun that had quit on the freeway. Though the car was in gear, when Maka leaned on the gas pedal she wouldn't go, as if in neutral.

Neutrality is especially hard to come by when the people you know are being shot at by people whom you don't know. One of the many moral ambiguities of war. Right and wrong get more and more blurry, finally indistinct. It took Maka an entire week in Nam to catch on to this; another week to fall victim. Maka had tried but failed to be the objective camera eye he thought he could be in Nam. The objective camera eye he had prided himself to be in film school, even when discussions focused on the subjectivity that is superimposed on everything we do, and every response. Maka and Walker argued about that a lot. It drove Walker nuts whenever Maka hinted that film was a more objective medium than written journalism. And because Maka knew it drove him nuts, he brought it up constantly.

The drive down Kalanianaole didn't even make him blink. He was too lost in fantasy. Looking at the elegant homes dotting the Koolaus, he thought *I'll make it work for Pualani and baby. I'll build a house with my own hands if I have to. We'll find our place in this Hawaiian sun. . . . Maybe the job ain't so bad, after all. It's civil service; I'd really have to fuck up for them to fire me. The bennies are good . . . medical . . . And once they learn how good I can handle a camera—not this stupid Polaroid, though—they might even let me do some A-V work. It's a big enough department. I can do so much better than those workshop people, those film-illiterates. Buy my own sixteen millimeter. . . .*

Smoke came out from under the hood as Maka blasted the horn to warn other cars, then pulled to the side of the freeway. He kicked the car with his good leg; it still hurt. He realized he had gone barefoot, as if Hawaii was truly making an imprint on him. He started running along the freeway's edge. *It's only about a mile and a half away.* His thigh began to hurt again. Bad.

There were two shots in Vietnam that Maka will never forget. Besides the one that hit his leg, there was the one that ripped through Amos Ledbetter's body and stole his soul. It wasn't the bullets that sprayed his body that Maka was thinking about; it was the shot that made him vulnerable to being shot. It was the photograph he had taken of Amos just moments before he was killed. Not that Amos minded. He, like many other chiefs, had not shared Jimmy's or, for that matter, Crazy Horse's belief about stealing one's shadow. Why, he had even smiled for the camera. But Amos had been a legend; there were stories told about him throughout I Corps, from Chu Lai to Danang to the DMZ. Bullets always missed him. He'd stand out in the open, shooting back at the enemy, seemingly invulnerable. Then there'd be quiet; *x* one

172

sniper. Moments after Maka had taken his picture, Amos was downed by a fusillade of sniper bullets. Amos. The one who seemed to see in infra-red. The one who could smell a gook.

"Gook?" Maka had said to him when he first heard Amos say that word with such venom. "They're fighting the same people, at least the same mentality, that wiped out your people not that long ago." College kid talk spewed out of him. "These people are fighting for their land. *Their* land. Why the fuck are we here?"

"Why the fuck are *you* here? What's *your* fucking problem?" he said, stalking away. "Why don't you go back to your safe world. Don't tell me about *my* people. You don't know who my people are. . . . You wouldn't know an Indian from Columbus. . . ."

"Yeah, I know them just about as well as you know your fucking gooks!" Though Maka was shouting, Amos had already disappeared into the all-consuming jungle. Then Walker came by.

"So why's us niggers here? That's what I wants ta know."

"I dunno," Maka said, walking away. He wasn't in the mood to kid around. He had seen his first dead "gooks," and he didn't think that was funny. Then he stopped, dead in his tracks, and turned around. He looked at Walker. "Somebody's got to clean up the mess. And you know we can't count on Puerto Ricans."

"Davis, youse one we-ird Me-sican."

An "Indian" had overtaken Maka as he hobbled in the late morning heat down the freeway. Maka had heard a rumbling, pulsating sound approaching from behind him and his first thought was to dive out of the way. It turned out to be booming speakers, coming out of a Toyota subcompact. This seemed to Maka to be the inverse equivalent of a 60's type transistor radio in a gym. Perhaps a more accurate description, Maka thought as he warily entered the car, was that this was the product of a marriage between a Walkman and a ghetto blaster, having inherited the worst traits of both parents.

This guy turned out to be someone who was already running quite late in going to work. He told Maka, once he had turned the car stereo down, but only a little, that he couldn't help but pick him up—he looked that pathetic.

"I pro'bly gon' get fired," he yelled. "But what da hey man. Sick a' da fucking boss."

"You can drop me off near the next offramp," Maka said, yelling too. "The Palama offramp."

"Hey, brah, no worry," the young Filipino shouted. "I take you whereva you gotta go. No worry 'bout me. I was figuring I gon' quit anyway. . . . What, you like I take you service station? Get one tow truck?"

"Nah. How about dropping me off by Tamashiro Market?"

"Shee brah. Your cah broke down an' you like go buy fish?"

"I just need to—" *The lei! Shit, I forgot the lei!* "Hey, uh, we gotta turn back. I forgot something important. I'll give you five bucks—ten, if you take me back."

"Hey brah, you not going crazy on me eh?" the young man said as he took the Palama offramp. "You not on drugs, eh?"

"No, no . . ." Maka figured that the truth would be too complicated and opted for a small lie. "I, ah, deliver flowers. I'm late for my last delivery. A lei. I forget it in the car . . . I can lose my job."

"Hey, brah. No need make up stories. If you gotta go back, I take you back. No worry," he yelled over the reggae sounds that pounded out a beat that Maka's good leg did triplets to, "we geff 'om."

The jeeps arrived at a gate. The chain had already been cut. It looked to Maka like a SWAT team had arrived, or a hit squad. Some of the men were uniformed. No information had been given —at least not to Maka. He couldn't help but think, *How often does this go on while we're sitting in our air-conditioned offices?* The grim entourage proceeded up a hill. Even if there was a threat up ahead, Maka pondered, isn't this a bit of an . . . Maka's thoughts were stopped hard by the view he now saw—a squalid row of houses; shacks actually, shelters, pieces of plywood slapped together, tarp. Maka then had a distant, vague memory of a Vietnamese hamlet. *But this isn't Vietnam, this is Hawaii.*

Then Bob, a fellow worker, a Chinese man with a hard face until he grinned, came up to Maka and said: "Your job is to take pictures of us posting eviction notices on the doors. This way we have proof that we gave them fair warning. Maka looked at the makeshift homes. *Doors?* He could scarcely distinguish doors.

Don't take my picture. Just don't. Just respect that just respect

174

that just respect . . . the Badlands, Vietnam, Kahoolawe, and now, this sorry mound of dirt on a cliff, all strung together like beads, like the lei Maka now pulled out of a car that had lost its shadow in the late morning sun, pulled out through the open window, running, as if from the law that would be there soon to shake its sorry head and impound, running, as if being pulled by external forces, thinking *Maka doesn't your name mean eye, Maka, doesn't your name mean eye of the needle? Maka, didn't you stumble upon that in a Hawaiian dictionary, Maka? Didn't you have to start buying your heritage back, first at the university, so afraid you were of being found out? Maka, who has strung through your camera eyes this horror movie, this fetid lei. . . .*

Maka snapped the pictures, like he had learned to do, like he had been told to do. He snapped. And as he dutifully recorded the posting of eviction notice after eviction notice, he thought: A department of the state, the department I work for, under the orders of faceless men, had come to this hallowed piece of ground in the guise of a SWAT team, to warn some Hawaiians to get off what a page from an IBM ream told them was state land . . . and my job is to record it.

And he did.

Snap. More of a *click* actually, followed by a *jhhhhhh* — instant printing. Not like the *shhhhht-tk-tk-tk* sound of good cameras. *Click, jhhhhh.* Two houses down. *Click, jhhhhhh.* Three. And so on. Record, he thought. Record all this. You can use this against *them* one day. But he knew better. He knew that he was only complying. *Complicity.* The word reverberated. Stung. *Click, jhhhhhh. Click, jhhhhhh.* Maka wiped off his sweaty forehead. *Damn, these cheap cameras. Good only for seedy amateurs who take unflattering nude shots of their lovers, failing to capture, steal, their essence.*

Then an elderly Hawaiian man came out from one of the shacks, weeping. "Why you cannot leave us alone? Dis all we have. What harm we goin' do up heah away from ev'ret'ing, eh?" *Click, jhhhhhh.* Maka got that one too. Then something in him went *shhhhht-tk-tk-tk.*

Maka rode back silent, numb. He didn't go to work the next day. Nor the next. Nor the one after that. He didn't take the calls from the office. He ripped up the last paycheck they mailed to him. And came to regret it when the eviction notice came to *his* house.

The young Filipino dropped Maka off at Tamashiro Market. He wouldn't take a ten, but took a five. *Mayday. Mayday.*

Maka rushed across the street, the lei firmly in hand. He didn't see any sign of an event; the school seemed silent, deserted. He limped toward the administration building, sweating in the late morning heat. He began to panic. *Mayday. Mayday.* He started running, ignoring the pain shooting up his left thigh. He looked down one of the two corridors that met together, forming a V. He looked down the left corridor, then down the right. He chose the right. He ran blindly, trying to follow his ears, his sense of smell, stumbling, the heat and exhaustion now catching up. As he reached what seemed to be a dead end, he heard the faint sound of children's voices and thought, *The back! They're in the field in the back!* He ran down another corridor, the one that led to the parking lot. The voices were getting louder, louder!

And then he turned the corner. Maka stopped short as his eyes were stabbed first by the brightness of the sky, then by the stunning array of the *'a'ai* colors he saw, an artist's orgy of colors. Not just the *uli* of the night sea and Vietnam and bruises, those dark greens and blues that offer no relief, but the *melemele* of bright stars, the *'ula* that begins for us the *anuenue* that arcs through the sky. Maka saw a painting, a photograph that had no rival in its casting of light and commiserate joy. *May Day.* He heard happy voices as he stumbled toward the sparse gathering, the lei held more loosely now. He worked toward the colors, the *mu'umu'us,* the aloha shirts, worked his way toward the front as the *keiki* voices grew louder, stronger, more together:

E Hawaii e kuu one hanau e, kuu home kulaiwi ne
Oli no au i na pono lani ou, E Hawaii aloha e. . . .

Maka's heart sank. He had enough familiarity with the song to get chicken skin, though he didn't know what the words meant. *Mai na aheahe makani e pa mai nei. . . .* He also had enough familiarity with the song to know that it was sung last, at the end of an event. He had blown it. Then he jumped; someone had jabbed his ribs. He turned around and saw Pualani, beautiful in a lavender

176

holoku that matched her eyes.

"Sorry, I—" he started to say.

"My god, you're a mess!"

"I'm sorry about missing the program." He held up the lei.

"Wha' do you mean, missing the program? They haven't started yet."

"But they're singing 'Hawaii Aloha.'" The singing stopped.

"They were doing one final rehearsal! Oh, Maka." She pressed her head against his chest. Then she looked up at him. "God, you're a mess! Look what I brought." She held up his old Canon.

"Where'd you find that?"

"Never mind. Wanna trade?" Maka looked at the lei.

"No way . . . where's baby?"

"Coming up right behind you. She's spotted us."

Maka whirled around, pivoting on his bad leg. As he whirled his daughter leaped. He caught her in mid-air, her momentum spinning him around, his bad leg digging deeper and deeper into the grass, into the earth, he gazing up at her face, a bright *kama'ehu* tanned face against the *malamalama, polu* sky. "I love you, daddy," she said, this *keiki* in her *mu'umu'u.* The swirling, the digging in, continued. Pualani began snapping photographs. *Shhhhht-tk-tk.*

"Where'd you park?" Pualani asked. He didn't answer. *Shhhhht-tk-tk-tk.*

"Come on, you two; enough is enough. The program's about to begin." *Shhht-tk-tk, shhhhht-tk-tk-tk.*

177